I0520174

Praise for

Viva Zapata & the Magic 8-Ball

"This story gave me goose bumps when it was still in the plot stage. Verte's debut title, Viva Zapata & the Magic 8-Ball, is more than another feel good tale. It is engaging, emotional, and leaves you curious to find what your own journey is really all about."

-Cherry Adair, New York Times Bestselling Author

*****

"When reading this story, I was able to identify with so many of the characters. There is something in these women that I think everyone will see a little of themselves."

-Jolanthe Aleksander, Author
Beyond the Veil of Whispered Dreams

SAVANNAH VERTE

Viva Zapata

&

the

Magic 8-Ball

SAVANNAH VERTE

Viva Zapata & the Magic 8-Ball

By Savannah Verte

Published by
Eclectic Bard Books
USA

This novel is a work of fiction. Any resemblance to actual persons, living or deceased is coincidental. The characters, names, plots, or incidents within are the product of the author's imagination. References to actual events or locations are included to give the fiction a sense of reality.

Copyright 2015, Savannah Verte

All rights reserved. No part of this may be reproduced, stored, or transmitted in any form, by any means without written consent from Savannah Verte.

Cover design, The Book Lady 2015.

ISBN: 978-0692493861 (Trade Paperback)

For the Zapatistas out there everywhere,

whatever challenges you are trying to overcome…

Viva La Revolution!

SAVANNAH VERTE

With Gratitude

To the incomparable Cherry Adair who helped me figure out how to tell this tale.

To Cabana, Weese, Whitehead & Young who were instrumental in the journey to realizing the dream.

To Magic 8 who said *'It is certain'.*

To family, friends, the writing community, and those who kept cheering.

Most of all, to the readers.

SAVANNAH VERTE

'Learn from what was,

Embrace what is,

Plan for what will be.'

—unknown

SAVANNAH VERTE

Concentrate and ask again

Two fears collided as Abi Stewart rounded the corner of baggage carousel seven at McCarran airport. The first was a deep, long standing fear that her friends had not come and she would once again be standing alone. The second surprised her as a new insecurity reared up and stole her breath. It was a nervous fear as she looked up and noticed the three beauties at the far end. Not only had they come, but these were her companions for the weekend.

A lose or lose notion reared its ugly head and threatened to wipe the smile from her face. She forced herself to breathe through her nose as she held her grin in place and started toward the trio. The returning radiant smiles confirmed fear number two of the morning. She would not be standing alone, they were here, and this was them.

Her father had always told her that achieving greatness begins with the smallest disciplines. She had often found that keeping her composure in spite of her internal struggle required immense discipline. This time would be no exception.

Why she did this to herself was anyone's guess. In the span of distance from one end of the baggage wheel to the other she had assessed her clothing as inferior, inspected her makeup in her mind, and determined she needed better shoes. The queen of self-sabotage had evidently come along for the girl's weekend too. It was not without great effort that she managed to arrive where the others stood with her smile still in place.

"You all failed to mention that you were gorgeous." Abi began, hoping to move past her own feelings of awkwardness quickly with humor.

The tan, brunette, Marilyn Monroe curve twin, who had to be Margo, scoffed it off while the petite, maybe size zero soaking wet Meredith, blushed quietly. Only Dani, who actually was a model, looked bored and put off by the assessment and her opening volley. "Puh-leeze."

Abi tried humor again. "I'm just saying it so it's been said. I've seen your faces, but damn, really? You might have warned a girl."

Meredith chimed in, "I think you made my day. Are we set?"

"No, haven't seen my bag drop yet. You guys been here long?" Abi asked.

Dani was busily bopping her head and bouncing a hip making an 'Nnn-cha' sound over and over again as she swayed back and forth. Abi wasn't sure if it was code for, 'Yes we have. No, I'm bored.' Or 'Let me know when we're ready to move, I can't stand still.' Then again, it almost seemed like she was rocking out to a song only she could hear, Abi certainly couldn't.

Margo finally answered, breaking Abi's stare at the blonde amazon gyrating in front of her. "Nah, not long. I just arrived a bit ago actually. These two were already here, though I nearly missed Meredith for the group around them when I landed."

Meredith rolled her eyes. "Ha. Ha. Notice she didn't say she nearly missed 'us', just me."

Abi's eyes were wide. "Were you really surrounded?"

Meredith thumbed toward the six foot plus blonde to her left in jeans, t-shirt and a straw hat. "Even dressed like that they swarmed her. Not us…her. I just happened to be next to her." She giggled before continuing. "I almost got impaled by a pen being shoved at her." Meredith turned her shoulder out to show where a long streak of ink marked the back side of her arm from a random autograph seeker. "I could never live like this."

"Whoa." Abi turned to Dani after seeing the ink mark battle scar on Meredith. "How do you stand it Dani?"

Dani stopped bouncing for a minute and appeared to consider the question before she finally shrugged it off. "What choice do I have? It's how I earn a living."

Abi noted that Dani's voice was flat and resisted the urge to say she felt sorry for her. It was a choice after all. Not one she would make, but evidently it was a compromise that Dani was willing to live with.

"I get that, but still…a girl's got to get a break sometime."

Dani laughed out loud. "That's a nice idea Abi, just not really my reality."

Abi turned toward the baggage carousel as Dani's frown just might make her sad to keep watching. She focused on the wheel turning. When the cycle was complete, she concentrated a little harder watching it go around again. She had not seen her bag in the mix. Her inner voice started the alarm that she could not quite voice yet. She had one change of clothes and a spare toothbrush in the bag she had carried on and it was nowhere near good enough for their night out tomorrow night. She reminded herself not to panic and gave herself a stern inner command, *Whatever you do, do not start to cry.*

Meredith moved to her side as she watched the bags continue to turn round. "What does yours look like, I'll help you grab it."

"Thanks. I don't see it." Abi responded desolately.

"You sure they said seven?"

Abi shrugged. "I thought so, just a minute."

She went to the board and double checked for her flight. Carousel seven was assigned to her arrival. The bag should be here. She had been to the airport and checked her bag, plus gotten a coffee and a spot at the charging counter at her gate a full two hours before departure. There was no last minute run that would account for it missing the flight.

"Yes, it says seven." She muttered as she returned.

"Okay, we'll give it a little bit before we go find someone. Maybe there's another cart to unload. It looks like a few other people are still waiting too." She smiled as she nodded down the row between the carousels.

"I hope you're right. That, or we'll have to go shopping. There's no way I'm wearing this out tomorrow night."

Meredith's smile grew. "Oh, we're going shopping anyway. There's a great outlet mall at Stateline. We decided while we were waiting. Hope you brought money to spend and not just to lose gambling."

"Oh I never gamble."

"Never?"

"Nope. Never."

Meredith's jaw dropped. "Really…never?"

Abi snorted. "No. Never, not once. For my luck it'd be simpler to toss it down the toilet. At least that way I don't get my hopes up."

Meredith laughed and sat on the edge of the carousel while they waited. Abi stood watching the crowd. Another throng had encircled Dani at the far end. Craning to see, Abi could not tell if Margo was in the midst of the crowd this time. She thought it would be funny if she were after her earlier assessment of Meredith being swallowed up. She kept that to herself.

Hearing another bag drop, she turned back to see if hers was coming, catching Margo sitting in a chair off to the side as she did. It was only after she turned fully that she absently noticed and had to turn back to confirm what she thought she had seen. Margo was sitting with her leg propped up. Her foot, ankle, and lower leg were all firmly encased in a stabilization boot. *That can't be good.* She thought as she watched more bags fall.

Thirteen bags later, Abi's brown suitcase finally came down the chute. She nearly sank with relief. She had brought spending money, but not so much as to invest into a new wardrobe for Vegas clubbing.

"That's me." She said pointing to the piece as it approached them.

Meredith jumped up and snatched it before Abi could, surprising her with the ease that she hefted the awkward bag.

"Whoa, you got some muscles hiding in your pocket." Abi snickered.

Meredith grinned wide. "Don't let my size fool you. I'm a tough-nut with strength to spare. Really, how many of us are actually what we seem?"

Abi wished she had a glass to raise but lifted her cupped hand in mock toast anyway. "Preach it sister!"

Meredith's smile faltered slightly. "Not gospel I'm sure, but the truth as I know it. Now let's get out of here."

"Deal!"

They moved together to the end area, head canting Margo to head over as they went to rescue Dani. Meredith shoved her way into the near inner circle of autograph hounds before raising her voice loudly.

"Danica is now off the clock folks. We have an appointment. Catch her next time."

Dani's face seemed a mix of relief and astonishment as the crowd moved off grumbling when Meredith seized her by her upper arm and pulled her from the crush of bodies. It was only after they were clear that Meredith's tone changed from all business to mocked ribbing.

"Lead the way Jeeves, where'd you park the car?"

Abi could hardly believe what she'd just seen and was out of breath from laughing so hard when the group was all standing together. Meredith, for all of her five foot nothing, looking moderately proper in her silk shirt, pearls, and blue jeans had just sent a crowd of two dozen packing. Abi made a mental note not to mess with Meredith.

Better not tell you now

Meredith had hopped into the seat behind Margo, leaving the one behind Dani for Abi. Margo had made a beeline for shotgun, started the engine, and begun fiddling with the radio while the other three loaded the bags into the back of the tricked out black SUV. Meredith was neither impressed nor pleased by the choice, or the volume. She rolled her eyes at Abi.

"Can you turn that down? Or off?" she said toward the front seat.

"You don't like it? Should I put on the tabernacle choir?"

Margo retorted smartly.

"Low blow Margo. Please just shut it off." Meredith was quickly losing her sweet disposition.

Dani reached behind her groping for a bag on the floor. "I know, we'll ask Magic 8."

Three heads swiveled around to stare at Dani, whose expression was completely serious, as she retrieved a Magic 8-ball from the bag and began to shake it.

Margo was the first to find her voice. "Are you kidding me?"

"No. Not at all." Dani countered still shaking furiously. "Seems to me that we are going to have these odd little things come up, so I brought a neutral fifth party to the gathering so there would be no tie voting."

Meredith looked from Abi's stunned face to Margo's nearly identical one before shrugging and speaking up. "What's the question? Don't you have to ask a question?"

Dani stopped shaking the ball. "You're right. Hmmm, the first question is..." she looked straight at the ball speaking completely calmly, "Magic 8, should we put on the Mormon Tabernacle Choir?"

Meredith rolled her eyes and watched as Dani resumed the fevered shaking from before. All four women leaned in as she stopped shaking, flipped it over, and waited for the answer.

Very Doubtful.

"Thank you Magic 8." Meredith said with a satisfied smile before leaning back in her seat.

Margo reached for the ball but Dani pulled it back. "Ask your question, I'll do the shaking. It knows me."

Wide-eyed, Margo jerked back, settled herself and finally spoke. "Okay then, Magic 8 should I turn the radio off or down?"

"You can't ask an either or question." Dani stated plainly.

Margo huffed. "Fine. Magic 8 should I turn the radio down?"

Reply hazy. Try again.

"Grrr. Magic 8 should I turn the radio off?"

As I see it, yes.

Meredith grinned in her seat, but didn't say a word.

Margo clicked the radio off, slammed her arms across her

chest, and crashed back against the seat. "Fine."

Dani put the Magic 8 on the steering console and checked the other passengers. "Anything else we need to ask or are we ready to go now?" Her face never faltered from serious.

"Move 'em out." Meredith chimed making a hatchet motion with her left arm toward the windshield.

Abi did a double take as Meredith's cap sleeve raised with the action, exposing what looked like a bodysuit underneath. Meredith pulled the sleeve back into place. "Ignore that, it's just my garments."

Abi mouthed back, "Care to explain that?"

"Not really. Maybe later."

They would be staying off Freemont Street at the Golden Nugget, so Dani took the scenic route down the main drag between the big hotels. Abi's eyes were wide as they passed one with a great big pirate ship and another with huge pillars and a stone front that was bigger than any football stadium she'd ever seen. Margo spun around at the sound of Meredith's laughter.

"Can't take the farm girl out of the Midwest huh?" Margo asked sounding amused looking at Abi.

"This is…yeah, uhm…big." Abi said with awe.

The vehicle erupted with laughter as the three shook their heads at Abi's assessment of Vegas.

"The rodeo is in town." Meredith finally explained when Abi commented again at the crazy number of people on the streets. "But, there is always a crowd here."

Dani was nodding from the front seat. "We'll steer clear of the MGM, that's bound to be a madhouse."

"And this isn't? They're walking around drinking." Abi said astonished. "It's like a people mill. There's hardly room between any one."

"Noooo, this is a tame, calm crowd. Vegas allows you to walk around with alcohol, that's not odd at all, but the rodeo is at the MGM so it will be significantly busier than this."

"Busier than this? Are you joking? Yes, let's steer clear of that then." Abi retorted. "Even if there are cowboys there."

Meredith was enjoying the back seat for a change. Abi was turning out to be one click away from pig-tails and short-shorts, and a riot at that.

Margo broke the quiet of Abi's gawking, "Where to first, the hotel, food, souvenirs?"

"Booze." Dani interjected. "I want to get some cocktails for the room, we can put them on ice when we check in."

Margo nodded. "Booze it is."

Several hours later they had finished the strip, driven the entire circumference of Vegas proper, found a liquor store and were in what appeared to be a neighborhood area.

"You guys want to stop now and eat, or go check in and then probably have to go back out? I don't know what's on Freemont for food." Dani asked over her shoulder while changing lanes between her intermittent 'nn-cha' thumping.

"There's nothing on Freemont for food beside the vendors if you don't want to eat in the casinos." Margo stated absently.

"Food's good. Where do you guys want to eat?" Meredith announced after Abi nodded but had said nothing. "There's a Macaroni Grill…"

"No…can't do the carbs." Dani decried.

"There's a Fridays right there." Margo was pointing.

"Fry-days…name says it all. Nope." Dani again dissented.

Abi finally spoke up. "We passed an Olive Garden about

two blocks back."

"I can do Olive Garden." Dani finally consented. "Okay by you two?"

Margo and Meredith shook their heads and shrugged. "That's fine." They said nearly together.

Meredith leaned in but pulled back before calling 'Jinx.' Somehow she was less certain about Margo's sense of humor live. They had joked often when they had all been chatting online, but in person things were feeling different.

Even though they were early, they had to wait for a table, and ended up in a far corner at an oversized round one when a four-top was going to take another ten minutes. They could have waited for the smaller table they decided in retrospect when it was easily another ten minutes before the waiter came, promptly asking Dani for her autograph and business card.

"Really? What are we, chopped liver?" Meredith fumed. "Dani is OFF the clock right now, contact her agent."

The waiter fumbled apologies, served water and asked if they were ready to order, skipping right over Meredith who was closest to him when he tried to start.

"Don't need the tips? Or just new? You are doing this wrong by the way." Meredith continued her tirade. "Why yes, we'd love drinks as a matter of fact, then you get our dinner orders."

The waiter was walking away, a bit battered looking as he headed toward the bar to retrieve drinks before anyone else spoke.

"That was a bit harsh don't you think? You come off all church-mouse in appearance but you're a hell-cat." Margo quipped.

"Oh my God…I mean gosh. Can we please forget the freaking church already? He was doing it wrong. If no one corrects him now he'll never learn. I appreciate that he's star-struck with Dani, but good grief, I did not come to Vegas to watch everyone we come into contact with get doe-eyed because she's in the room. No offense Dani." She said turning to Dani as she finished

"None taken. It's kind of nice for once to get to be a person instead of my job. Or, at least have someone try to make that happen for me."

"Do you think he'll mind then if I send him back to the bar before we get our meals? I'm going to need two drinks for this I think." Margo added out of left field.

Meredith dropped her forehead onto the table talking to the placemat. "Am I the only one who thought this was going to be like it was online?"

"What do you mean?" Abi asked. "In what way?"

"I don't know. It's just different in person." Meredith lamented, still talking with her face to the table.

"Of course it is, it has to be. We aren't online editing what we say or limited to the books. We're here now, and this is who we are. We just need to relax a little. I'm sure we're all travel-weary and on edge. We'll be okay." Abi consoled.

The table was quiet until later in the meal after everyone had done the initial inhale. None had realized how hungry they were until the food had arrived. Margo, Meredith and Abi all had dinners while Dani had soup and salad. She eyed but didn't grab a single breadstick, even refusing the one Meredith tried to put on her plate.

"You know one isn't going to kill you." Meredith stated.

"Yeah, it would. One leads to two, and two leads to twenty. I have no will power." Dani retorted.

"No will power, are you kidding me? You're a beacon of

will power to say no to breadsticks in my book." Meredith said sounding dismayed as she realized how many she herself had eaten.

Dani laughed. "Carbs, sweets, carbonated beverages, you name it, and it's off limits if I want to work."

Abi gave a wicked grin, "But alcohol is an exception right?"

"Alcohol is an exception for this weekend. After that, nope, it's off the list too."

"So, the other stuff can't be an exception? Abi questioned.

"Alcohol is easy not to buy, food is a harder battle since a girl has to eat. It's a slippery slope for me. I'm sure I'll cave, but I'm saving my caving for something good."

Margo huffed, "You say all that like having curves is such a bad thing."

The waiter returned with four desserts just then.

"We didn't order these." Margo said reaching for a slice of cheesecake.

"With my apologies. I forgot I was working when I saw who was at my table."

Abi chuckled under her breath, "Looks like the slope just

got greased."

"Can I have mine to go? Dani grimaced with a hard groan.

"Thank you for this." Meredith added.

"I do apologize. Dani here is my ideal leading lady for the film I'm working on. I couldn't help myself."

"You're a film maker?" Meredith asked.

"Film maker, writer, all of the above. Mostly screenplays." He answered.

"How interesting, Abi here is a writer too, maybe she can help you." Meredith beamed at Abi as she spoke.

Abi choked. She spoke up after she took a sip of her water. "Uhhm, what are you working on?"

"It's a zombie apocalypse piece. To tell the truth, I'm really only working on the one screenplay."

"Ah, not really my thing but good luck." Abi said quickly.

"I'm going to do the film too. It's going to be huge. Set right here in Vegas. I didn't know Dani was around here." He commented excitedly.

"I'm not. We're here for the weekend." Dani groaned.

"Oh. Would you maybe think about it? Can I give you my card or can I have yours?" He tried again.

"I'll be honest..." she looked at his nametag "...Pete, I'm really not looking to do moving film, but thanks." Dani said plainly.

Meredith popped up and interjected as the conversation was feeling awkward, "Back to business now Pete. Check please."

Outlook not so good

They were bumped from the Golden Nugget to a hotel across the street. The room was nothing to write home about as they loaded in. Dani spent time blowing up her air mattress and rearranging the room while the other three got their things set up.

Margo paused "Dani, why do you have an air mattress? Hotel rooms do come with beds you know."

Dani stopped, weighed her words, and replied matter of fact but quietly. "Because my feet hang off most mattresses and I can't sleep like that. At home with Michael it's fine because he lets me sleep diagonally. I didn't suppose any of you would be as comfortable trying to sleep that way with me, so I brought the air mattress so no one would have to try."

Everyone wore blank faces at the explanation and suddenly has something else to do. Dani returned to her set up without further comment.

Margo flopped on the bed she and Meredith were going to share and removed the boot from her leg before rubbing gently up and down her calf. Abi watched from the corner of her eye, not wanting to stare. The mottling revealed an older wound that must have been gruesome.

"Margo, I don't mean to be crass, but what the hell did you do?" Abi finally couldn't not ask any longer.

"I fell down the basement stairs."

"All of them?" Abi asked astonished before she could stop herself.

"No. Just the first flight. It's not as bad as it looks. I was chasing the kids and tripped over the dog. Someone had left the gate open and down I went."

"Holy crap!"

"Yeah. I think it scared Chris more than it hurt me. He said he was sorry for days."

"Chris is?" Abi drew it out.

"My youngest son."

"Oh. How old is he?"

"He's seven."

"I'm sure it's hard for any kid to see mommy get hurt. Really tough at that age. You got pictures?" Abi enquired.

Margo fished in her bag for her phone and scrolled through several screens before handing it over. "Chris is in the middle."

"Cute. He's going to be a heartbreaker." Abi commented while flipping through a couple more images before handing the phone to Meredith. "And your daughter?"

"Sasha is ten. The little string bean in the back hiding is Jordan, he's eight."

"Sounds like a handful. Mine are older and independent now thankfully. I was losing my mind with two at that age. You must be so busy. You got kids Meredith?" she asked as she turned.

Meredith glanced up from the phone and turned to hand it

to Dani who was busily rustling through a suitcase of t-shirts. "Yes. I have three as well, but they're older too. Jamie is going to be the death of me yet."

"Why's that?" Abi wondered out loud.

"Because she's intent to follow a path I think I'm leaving. I don't know if it's choice or rebellion and with the next birthday she's eighteen and has made it clear I won't have any say at all." Meredith lamented.

Margo gave a knowing 'hmm' but made no other comment.

"Oh. Good luck with getting a straight answer on that. You turned out all right though, what could be so bad about following your path?" Abi asked, again forgetting her filter.

"Trust me, I wouldn't if I could do it over. I don't want her making the same mistake. I'm still undoing mine."

"Meaning?"

"Meaning it's a long story." Meredith once again shut Abi down.

"Okay then." Abi turned to Dani who was sliding into a clean pair of jeans. "You're quiet over there."

"Nah, just doing. Got no kids to add to the conversation."

Dani said plainly as she moved to the dresser where the makeshift bar was set up. She poured herself a vodka and cranberry over ice before continuing. "We about ready to head out or what?"

Abi jumped up to change and Margo began putting the boot back on. Meredith frowned as she spoke. "I'm going to need a few minutes." she disappeared into the bathroom with a change of clothes. Margo didn't seem to notice and Dani poured another drink leaning against the table waiting.

"You sure you should be hoofing it with the boot Margo?" Dani finally said when the room was quiet and Meredith still hadn't emerged.

"I'll be fine. This is not the worst that's happened to me and probably not the last either. I can do this."

It was warm for November as they made their way onto Freemont Street amid the tourists and vendors. Meredith had come out dressed in a fresh silk shirt and jeans sans the pearls from earlier, but looking every bit as proper and refined. Only Margo had not changed clothes, though she was easily as dressed for the evening as any of them.

They stopped at a street cart and bought yarders before weaving through the stands of scarves, hookahs, tattoo artists and jewelry. In front of one of the casinos a showgirl was standing in full costume taking photos. Meredith pushed her camera and bag into Dani's hand with a 'Take my picture quick' but had to come back to get money since the woman in costume was charging for posing. Dani handed the bag and camera off to Abi when a group came up and wanted her picture at the same time.

The canopy over Freemont was lit with names of soldiers and 'I'm proud to be an American' was blasting loudly over a sound system. There were cowboys everywhere. Abi noticed, more than a little thankful they weren't all at the MGM. Dani was busy humming a different tune but kept losing her place when the sound system started the chorus again.

"You'd think they'd at least rotate the music." she complained. The canopy isn't changing, shouldn't the song?"

A half blitzed man came up to her asking for her photo and an autograph, but only if she could strip down to her bikini for it, she had on too many clothes. Abi was aghast.

"No, you cannot have my photograph or autograph. I'm off." Dani snapped.

"You did it for them other guys, I saw you. You stuck up? Too good to take a picture with me? Or are you just a bitch?"

he charged angrily.

"Yeah that's it. I'm a dumb blonde who is only good posing in a swimsuit, or I'm a bitch. Keep moving." Dani retorted matching his tone.

Abi came over after the man flipped her off and stalked away. "Gosh that sucks. You still want to be out?"

"Of course I still wanna be out." Dani flashed her best cover smile at Abi. "He's just another car."

"Pardon?"

"My life is all the same stoplight sweetie, it's just different cars."

"Well somebody needs to take him to the crusher." Abi stated.

Dani laughed. "If it were only that easy."

Meredith and Margo caught up to them after seeing the flip off from across the street where they had stopped to window shop.

"What did we miss?" Meredith asked.

"Yesterday's news." Dani replied. "Not worth a re-read."

"Speaking of yesterday's news, come 'ere. You have got to see this." Meredith grabbed Dani's arm as she had in the airport and drug her across to where she and Margo had been. On the newsstand in the window among the magazines was one with Dani on the cover. Meredith handed her camera to Abi. "Here, take our picture."

Margo was inside behind the glass pointing to the magazine and Meredith was standing next to Dani pointing to the live version. They were all grins, though Dani's looked a little pained, as Abi stood back from the group to take the picture without further comment. A few passers-by noticed the event and tried to stop Dani for autographs but got Meredith's hand in their face as she ushered Dani past them with a 'She's OFF'.

They moved on then to a gift shop. Abi spent time walking the aisles looking for gifts while the other three took pictures by the card board cutouts. Dani came up after a bit to see what she had found.

"Sorry. We've all been here before and this is not new for us. Are you finding anything good?"

Abi shrugged it off. "I am and I'm not. A lot of it is so gimmicky tourist stuff. I don't want to be 'that mom'."

"That mom? I'm not, so I don't know what that means. Want to explain?"

"Oh come on Dani...you know, 'My mom went to Vegas and all I got was this t-shirt' kind of stuff. Didn't your folks do that to you?"

"No. That's not what they did to me." She replied quietly already having said more than she planned. "Let's find you some 'not that mom' stuff."

Together they found a second floor that had some less gaudy things. Abi picked out beach towels, book bags and a couple lanyards before they grabbed a video of the water show on DVD from the main strip that they'd passed earlier and called it done. They rejoined the others at the bottom of the stairs and headed out.

A fresh set of yarders later, Dani announced that she had a surprise for everyone and they needed to drop stuff off. They piled into a cab and headed back toward the main drag. Margo once again had claimed the front seat.

My sources say no

Abi's jaw dropped as they pulled up in front of The Venetian with its waterway and gondolas. It was impressive. The doorman even got her door which wasn't happening at the hotel they were staying at.

As they walked the long hall toward the casino floor they passed several shops. She diverted into one that specialized in chain maille clothing, eyeing a top on the far wall. Lifting it, the thing weighed a ton. The weight wasn't what made her drop it though, the price tag was a cool three thousand dollars, quite a bit beyond her spending spree money for the weekend.

Dani led them through the casino to elevators on the far end. They climbed into a car and rode to the 12th floor. Down a short hall, Dani stopped and knocked on 1247. Abi waited for an explanation, none came.

The door opened and grinning back across the threshold at the group of them was Raven and Vera, also from the self-proclaimed book club where they had all met. Abi couldn't help it, she squealed.

"OhMyGods! Is it really you?"

Raven laughed between gasping for breath in the tight bear hug of the group. Vera had managed to be behind her and got her hugs separately. "Yes, it's really us. You didn't think we'd let you do Vegas without us did you?"

"But why aren't you staying with us?" looking around the room Abi rephrased, "Or, why aren't we staying with you?"

"It was a last minute surprise from my husband. I couldn't hand it back and say 'wrong hotel' could I? Don't you fret, I'll be with you for all the fun stuff." Raven replied over giggles.

The room was opulent, a real retreat dream. Big plush looking beds, a quick glance to the right revealed a deep soaking tub, and at the far end by the windows was a sunken living room with a huge sectional sofa. The group moved past the hugging stage to the seating area and the conversation went up for grabs.

Raven had spent time getting a massage and had some primo bath salts from the spa that were passed around. Vera was back and forth with family nearby but would be joining up again to go out with them tomorrow night. For a group of only six women, it was a busy conversation. Abi could hardly keep track of any of the exchanges and started taking pictures.

As soon as she began, other cameras and phones were being handed to her to take photos too. She fought the kick up feeling of being left out, trying to wait for her turn. She was with them, but she felt like she stood apart.

When it came time that someone else took a camera so she could get in the shot, she found Meredith leaning in to get a close up with her which shoved the anxiety away. Looking around the room she couldn't help but notice that she was surrounded by gorgeous women. She looked herself up and down in the reflection of the window glass before forcing herself to look at someone else. These were her friends, the rest didn't count.

There was a loud conversation going on as Margo was rehashing the boot. Abi noticed that this time she said she tripped while caught up in the leash chasing the dog, twisting it when she went down. If anyone else noticed the difference, they didn't react.

It was easily an hour into their catching up and chatting when there was a loud knocking on the door. Raven went to answer it, but everyone else turned to see who it was. Abi half expected more women from the 'book club'. That anticipation faded fast. Opening the door, on the other side stood a burly, bulky, Venetian security guard and his Barney Fife sidekick.

"There has been a complaint that there is a party going on in this room and it is too loud. I need you ladies to keep it down" The larger guard began.

"Holy shit Blake, it's Danica Marvel." Barney chimed in.

Dani sighed, turned, and put her head in her hands. "Fabulous, just what I need."

Raven nodded to the larger guard. "We didn't realize it was that loud. We'll quiet down. Thanks for coming by." She started to close the door. Barney was leaning to watch Dani as the opening diminished and Raven wiggled her fingers in a parting wave. Blake got his last words in sternly before the click, "See that you do."

Raven was rolling her eyes as she returned to the seating area. "Were we that loud? Good grief, it's not that late."

"I certainly didn't think so. It's Vegas for crying out loud." Margo stated. "Guess if what happens in Vegas is supposed to stay in Vegas, they need to have thicker walls than at The Venetian."

The chorus of laughter was loud in response. Only Dani was still cringing from the exchange.

"You gonna be okay?" Vera asked her from across the table.

"Yeah. As long as this doesn't hit the newswire and get to my agent. I really don't need the lecture about public behavior."

"Ugh. I bet."

Abi was still snickering, trying not to bust out laughing again, muttering "Thicker walls…ohmygod Margo!"

The laughter rose as they all joined in, even Dani finally giggled and relaxed again. They debated going down to the bar, seeing a show, or finding something else to do between peals of laughter from different voices.

Another loud knocking on the door sealed the deal. They

needed to go somewhere else. All six grabbed their bags as Raven reached the door, stating loudly before opening it, "We know, we're going out now." When she opened the door, no one was there.

Margo connected again. "And we were inconsiderate?" The snickers continued down the hall to the elevator but didn't erupt into laughter until after the polished double doors clicked closed.

As they wandered around the main floor, they found the sports bar was open, but the seating area was empty. Grabbing drinks, they all pulled up chairs ramshackle fashion and sat to chat in a misshapen circle. The chitchat was idle for a bit, but then it came out in mad clumps as if they were still sitting upstairs commiserating.

Margo wandered back and forth to a row of slot machines, dropping coins, pulling the lever, cursing, and walking back to listen to other conversations but not really joining any. Vera was talking about going back to school and trying to move and balance keeping her kids busy. Margo was nodding along at the comments about how hard it is to juggle everything with kids. Raven too was talking about kids having just become a new grandmother. Abi about swallowed her tongue. She could not fathom Raven being old enough to be a grandmother.

Dani had gotten another drink and sat down next to Abi opposite Meredith who was politely listening to the other ladies.

"Do you think I'm dumb?" Dani finally spat out after taking a long drink of her screwdriver.

"Good gods no, why would you ask that?" Abi replied, quietly abhorred.

"Call it insecurity. Everyone only sees the outside."

"Oh Dani no. You aren't dumb. You also are not your waistline, your amazing blonde hair, your clothes, or lack of clothes in some cases. I'm sorry if my 'gorgeous' comment at the airport was upsetting. I was trying to be funny. I felt pretty outclassed looking at you three."

"What?! Why?" Dani's eyes were huge in shock.

"Call it insecurity. I only see the reflection." Abi shrugged it off.

"Touché." She lifted her drink in salute before taking another long draw.

"I'm not paranoid or anything." Abi commented. "I am a

realist though. And, I pay attention. I think we all have a little something like that going on that we aren't talking about. There have been quite a few awkward things today."

"You got that too huh?" Dani lifted a brow emphasizing the question

"Oh yeah."

"Good. I thought it was just me."

"No, not just you, and I'd be willing to bet it's not just us either." Abi said motioning back and forth between them.

"So you're saying we're all equally flawed?"

Abi chortled. "We're all in Vegas because we met reading books online. Really? You think there's not a typo in this tale?"

Dani's grin was wide. "A typo is this tale?" she shook her head smiling. "You are such a writer."

"If wanting to be counts, then I guess I am." Abi shrugged.

"You are."

"I'll take that as a compliment."

"You should."

"Thanks Dani. I needed that."

"I think that's how it works."

"How what works? Lay it on me Ms. Marvel."

Dani mock punched Abi. "How friendship works silly. You are supposed to support the dreams of the ones you count as friends. Even if they aren't the same as yours."

"I think you are incredibly wise Dani. You do a mean gorgeous blonde impersonation though." Abi returned the punch.

"Smartass."

"Better than a dumbass. Abi mocked.

"Or a dumb ass blonde." Dani continued the banter.

"You'll never be a dumb blonde to me." Abi tried to convey how sincere she was but pulled back before the stupid tears she could seldom control started. She swallowed them back before continuing. "So, not dumb blonde, what's your dream?"

Dani's grimace was mixed with melancholy that she stuffed down. "I want what everyone wants Abi...what I don't have."

"Why do I think we are standing on the edge of a deep well?"

"We probably are. We should drink more." Dani jumped up and headed to the bar holding up a finger questioning if Abi needed a refill.

Abi roared and called after her. "Nice diversion. Yes please."

Meredith turned then, "Diversion from what?"

"Oh we were just discussing the meaning of life. She bailed on me." Abi laughed.

Meredith's eyes were wide. "You're joking right?"

"Yes, I'm joking. We were commenting that there is a lot more to each of us than what we see on the surface."

"Such as?"

"Oh…insecurities, hot buttons, and things we are being careful not to talk about, or actively hide while we're here. We know each other but we don't." Abi ticked off a rough list with her fingers.

"Do you think that will change?"

Abi hesitated. "I think we will know each other better for

being here, but I don't know that it will really change much unless we want it to. We have different lives away from here that we aren't necessarily sharing."

Meredith harrumphed her response with a slight frown while considering the statement. "I think that makes me sad."

"Sad? Why sad?"

"In some ways you guys have become my closest friends. In others, there are people that know me better, but aren't as close to me personally, they just live closer. It's kind of sad to think that those I would call better friends know less than those who are only proximal."

Dani returned with the drinks as Meredith finished. She sat down without saying anything, only listening to the comment as she sipped her fresh cocktail. Abi took her refill from Dani before responding. "I never would have expected such philosophy while drinking in Vegas. It might give Sin City a bad reputation if this became a thing."

Abi got mock punches from both sides before she could back pedal. "Okay, okay...geeze. I'm just saying that this isn't what I expected. I'm not upset to get to know you guys better. I guess I thought conversation would be books or something more trivial." She rubbed her arms, "Dang, y'all better not be leaving bruises, I got no sleeves tomorrow night."

Dani rolled her eyes. "I have make up. I can cover anything."

"Somehow that doesn't really make me feel better."

Yes

Margo's phone rang no less than five times in the cab ride from The Venetian back to their hotel. Meredith's foot bounced harder with each ring as they heard her side of each call.

"I just bought dogfood this week…did you check the pantry? Yes, I'm sure. Look again."

Meredith switched legs, bumping her foot against Dani in the middle of the back seat. "Oh, sorry."

"It didn't hurt."

Meredith sank her shoulders and sighed out loud with the

next ring, slouching into the seat.

"No, it's not in a bag, it's a stack of cans. Have Jordan show you. No, put your father on the phone."

Dani began her 'Nnn-cha, nnn-cha, nnn-cha' bouncing, shoulder bumping between Abi and Meredith. "Sing it with me."

"Sing what, there are no words." Meredith replied testily.

"You don't need words, come on. Nnnnnnn…" Dani looked imploringly at Meredith who rolled her eyes and spat back, "CH."

Back at the room the calls continued. Meredith's temper escalation did as well. Margo had just gotten her boot off and into shorts and a t-shirt when her phone rang again.

"Can't they live one night without you? It's after midnight for crying out loud. Shouldn't they be sleeping or something?" Meredith sounded off

Margo waved her off and went to stand in the hallway leaving the door ajar. The sound carried through anyway. Meredith collected her things and went into the bathroom once again to change.

Dani flopped on the edge of Abi's bed, grabbed the remote,

and flipped on the television. After the plethora of pay per channels they finally got to the normal broadcast stations. So late at night, there wasn't much on.

Dani and Abi both changed into loungewear and were absently watching the television talking when Meredith emerged. She was dressed in long sleeve silk pajamas with pants to match. She sat on the side of the bed after putting her clothes away and began rubbing herself down with lotion from the bottom up. She did her feet, legs, hands, and arms before switching to night cream and doing her face too. Abi and Dani watched her and had stopped talking.

"What? It's just lotion. The air here is dry." She finally commented.

"No one said a word Meredith." Dani defended. "Are you okay?"

She huffed glancing at the door still ajar with Margo in the hallway. "Ugh, someone close the freaking door. I know she's got kids, but dang really? This is supposed to be OUR time. I've got kids too, so do you," she looked at Abi "and we aren't on the phone constantly."

Dani had turned to watch the television. "Hey, I know this show."

Meredith grabbed a key, walked to the door, handed it to Margo and closed it before sitting back down. "What show are you watching?"

"Well that was abrupt." Abi commented.

"I just need a few minutes. Tell us about your show Dani." Meredith huffed.

"It's Viva Zapata! Mmmmmmm, young Brando."

"I got Brando out of that." Abi joked trying to lighten things up. "Care to translate the rest?"

"Marlon Brando is Emiliano Zapata. He's like the confederate Poncho Villa. They are fighting against Diaz, who is a dictator, over land rights. They end up forming this revolution, which really backfires in the end, but it's for the right reasons. Hmmm, that's not quite clear huh?" She paused.

Okay, try it this way...he's like a Mexican Robin Hood. He's fighting to take back for those who have been taken from and oppressed by the government. He's got this guide Fernando, who's like Little J...no he's not. Anyway, they back a guy named Madero. They kind of win, but then they do what all great heroes do, they get ambushed and die."

"Guess we don't have to watch it then since you just gave us the cliff notes." Abi joked.

"It's almost over anyway, but it's a great story."

"Sounds like a good movie." Meredith added. "Young Brando you say?"

"It's not just a movie, he's a real guy. It's a true story. It's fictionalized, but it really happened. Here's a writer thing for you Abi, the movie is a metaphor."

"How so?" Abi prodded her to continue.

"Life is a revolution. It's a fight to become true to who you are against every rule, program, social stigma, routine, doctrine and instruction. For the movie, it's about the struggle against the overlord for land rights and to be rid of the oppression placed on them. For life, it is a struggle against apathy, animosity, entitlement, greed, opposition, indifference and the corruption of men by power...not for your land or belongings but for your life. What we don't fight for, we lose."

Meredith was sure she and Abi had the same blank stares on. They were both silent staring at Dani, who continued imploringly.

"What? It is. Tell me you don't have something that you are fighting for or against for the life you want? Tell me you don't dream of something different, something that maybe seems just beyond your reach."

Abi opened her mouth and closed it again. When she finally opened it to speak her finger went up in Dani's face. "Never again...do you ask me if I think you are dumb. Never. Do you hear me?"

Dani grinned as she beamed back with a single nod.

Meredith threw her hand in the air, "Viva Zapata!"

Dani nodded hard. "Viva la revolution!"

"Wow." Abi said, obviously still processing.

"Come on Abi, you know you want to...Viva Zapata!" Dani mocked.

Abi snorted out an astonished single sound before getting out, "Viva Zapata."

"So who's our Zapata?" Meredith asked.

"I think we all are. Or, we all are on our personal journeys anyway." Dani replied thoughtfully. "Or, maybe the journey itself is Zapata."

"Okay, so what are his followers called?" Abi wondered out loud.

"Crap. I could have told you until you asked. Lemme think a minute."

Meredith and Abi stared at Dani as she began her bouncing thing. Meredith was beginning to believe less that it was a nervous thing, and more that it was a thinking or coping thing that helped her concentrate. She was just about to ask when Dani's arms flew out, palms forward, fingers spread wide. Abi and Meredith both flinched backwards.

"They're called Zapatistas." Dani announced proudly.

"So, if we buy your metaphor," Abi questioned, "we're Zapatistas too?"

"Yes. Yes we are." Dani grinned. "I am anyway. I think you have to choose for yourself. I mean, he led the revolution, and he was the one ambushed and killed for it, but none of us makes it out of this life alive right? So what are we doing? I am fighting for a life…the one I want, not the one I've been handed."

"I can agree with that" Meredith chimed in, throwing up her hand again. "Viva Zapata!"

Abi was nodding her head, "Viva la Revolution! I'm in."

You may rely on it

Margo walked back in to the three of her companions shouting 'Viva Zapata!' and "Viva la Revolution!' with their fists in the air between fits of giggles. The walls here must be thicker she thought snidely. She'd heard them shouting for at least ten minutes and no one had come to knock.

Just as she closed the door, Dani shot up like a rocket and ran for the bathroom. Sounds of retching could be heard clearly through the door. Margo threw her fist in the air and made a beeline for Dani, adding her own, "Viva la bouncing around with alcohol on an empty stomach."

Reaching the bathroom door, she caught and stopped herself before turning the knob. This was not one of her kids or her patients. It was hard to stop short.

"Dani? Are you okay? Do you want me to come in?" she tested the handle quietly as she queried, just in case there was no response.

"No. Don't come in. I'll be fine." Came the labored, groaning response.

Margo debated the truth of the answer, deciding she would try again in a few minutes. She didn't want to be pushy. She had been worried all evening about Dani drinking on her soup and salad. She knew at dinner there was no way that was going to go well, but she already felt like she was dragging down the group with her boot and elected to remain quiet then. The air around the group was sticky enough at that point without her adding to the mix nagging Dani.

She went back to her side of the bed she was going to share with Meredith and sat down. She slipped her boot off once again and rubbed out the tingles that raced her leg.

"So what did I miss? What's with all the 'Viva' stuff?" she asked absently not looking up.

Dani called from the bathroom and asked for a clean shirt.

Meredith hopped up to grab one and disappeared into the bathroom. Margo looked at Abi blankly. "I would have gotten her one."

"I'm sure you would have. She probably wasn't ready for one yet." Abi replied flatly.

Margo wanted to believe that and tried to refocus.

"So…the 'Viva' stuff?"

"Ohhh, right, right. It was a show that was on. Dani could do the quick version better than I can, I haven't seen it. What I got is basically it's a movie that's supposed to be one of those deeper meaning things, an allegory if you will, for life's journey and the battle we each have. We decided we each have our own revolution to wage as we aren't where we want to be…so Viva Zapata is the movie, and Viva la revolution is the battle cry." Abi tried to sum up.

Margo laughed openly. "Well if that isn't the truth of it all in a nutshell. I always miss the good stuff."

"Yeah, I didn't tell it nearly as good as Dani did. It was better the first time."

"So can anybody join the revolution?" Margo asked quietly trying not to sound overly interested or disinterested at the same time.

"It's your revolution kiddo, we're all just here to support you if you make the fight."

"I have more battles to fight than I know how." Margo admitted before she stopped to filter herself.

Abi smiled softly. "Margo, I do think we all do. I think recognizing them is half of it though. I'm here to back you up. You know that right?"

Margo looked at Abi and gauged her sincerity before speaking. What she wanted to say could come out vulnerable or really harsh and she wasn't sure which way it was going to go. She'd been overly successful with harsh so far. It wasn't really working for her. She took a deep breath, locked her stomach down, and threw her heart into it.

"Then I guess I have a confession to make." She hoped she didn't sound as awful as she felt.

Abi's face said 'Oh?' but luckily she didn't speak, Margo was not sure she could get the nerve to say it again.

"I should apologize. I really didn't think you liked me much. I haven't tried to talk to you, or get to know you, or anything, even online. I felt like we were each in the group for one of the others and you weren't there for me."

Abi came around the bed and sat next to her. "Margo, we are different places in our lives. I wouldn't say that I don't like you. I have felt like I couldn't connect with you though. You are so busy all the time with raising your kids and running your house. I'm done with all of that. I feel ancient when I hear about everything you are doing. Maybe it's even that I envy you. I don't have half your drive or energy anymore. You're always running. You never miss anything as far as I can tell." She commented quietly.

"That's funny. I miss plenty. Look what all my drive and energy gets me?" Margo gestured to her leg. "This is busted up ankle number two in as many years."

Abi interrupted. "Number two?"

"Yeah. I got tripped up in the dog least the first time. I have the bones of a seventy year old, and longer healing time because I'm 'dietary deficient.' Margo remarked harshly, using her fingers to make air quotes to emphasize that she had been told these things, not just believed them.

"I have kidney stones because I forget to stop and drink a glass of water…you don't want what I have." At the end, her voice was sad sounding in her own ears. She kicked herself for the revelations. Surely Abi would not want to become closer to her or know her any better after finding out how damaged she really was.

Abi placed her hand on Margo's. Once Margo looked up at her she finally spoke again. "Let me ask you something then, because I know you only get to raise your kids once and the last thing you want are regrets. What do you want to be different? I see you. I hear you. You couldn't be a better mom if you were June Cleaver, so what do you want to be different?"

Margo spoke before she could stop herself. "I want my kids to be able to remember me as everything. Everything, except broken." She tried to make it seem less significant than it was.

"Then we need for you to not be broken."

"You say that like it's an easy thing. Abi. It's not."

"Oh I never said that. We are all broken in some way or another. I think you mean broken as in physically broken. That's what needs to change. So now the question is how."

Margo's phone went off. They both looked at the clock, it was after 2 am. Groaning she picked it up and paused before clicking to connect the call hoping Meredith couldn't hear it ringing.

"Save my spot, I gotta…"

"…do what you need to do." Abi finished with a head nod toward the door.

Margo grabbed a room key and the car keys from the dresser before ducking out, clicking answer as the door closed.

"Is the house on fire?" she began.

She didn't want to be snarky, she was just tired and feeling like she was missing out on her time with the girls. She made her way to the parking ramp and got in the passenger seat of Dani's SUV. The dark windows would help keep out any prying eyes and keep the conversation private.

She couldn't bring herself to sit in the hallway again. She kept wondering if her friends were listening from the other side of the door one minute, and the next wondering if they were having a better time without her judging from the giggles and shouting they were doing. She wasn't sure she wanted the answer either.

She knew Meredith was upset that she kept taking calls, but Meredith knew how important it was for her not to miss anything with her kids, even if it was only that they needed to hear her voice. How many times had she wished for something so simple when she was their age? Too many.

The call was quick. She was also promised it was the last one for the night. There was a debate over the order of the agenda for Saturday morning, which was important. They had it backwards which meant Chris would have been early for soccer and Sasha would have been late for lessons. She felt needed. It made the open wound hurt a little less at being away from them.

She stayed in the truck for a while thinking through what Abi had told her about the movie and revolutions, surprised to find she had Abi's support. She certainly hadn't earned it. She still didn't know how to make it work though, even with support. When she had gotten married and she had found out they were going to be parents the first time, she promised herself she would be everything and do everything to be the best mom in the world. It had nearly beat her more than once since.

The damaged ankle was just the latest in a long line of injuries or breaks, some requiring surgery. She had cried herself to sleep more than once worrying that her kids would always remember her as always being somehow broken. The thought alone should have driven her to change, but she couldn't see a way to do things differently than running at

220 with her hair on fire.

Spying the Magic 8-ball sitting in the console, she looked out both windows and the back to make sure no one was watching before she reached for it. She looked up through the windshield too before bringing it up to level just to make sure she wasn't on a security camera either.

"I know, you're Dani's…but I need an answer too, just for me. So it'll be our little secret that I touched you okay?"

She shook her head snorting, not believing that she was talking to a Magic 8-ball like it was a living thing. She debated putting it back and calling it a night, deciding to just give it one shake. One shake couldn't hurt.

"Can I do this?" she asked out loud and shook the ball like Dani had earlier, flipping it over waiting for it to settle. She had to lean against the window to get enough light to see the answer without turning on an overhead light. *Reply hazy. Try again.*

"I guess that wasn't very specific. Okay, let's try this one…Can my family survive the weekend without me?" she asked.

Outlook good.

"Good enough." She said to the ball before returning it to the console near the shift where she had found it. She vacillated a few moments longer on how to do anything more than she was doing. She hoped as she hopped out of the truck that the answers were just where she should be, sleeping.

She made her way back to the room, checking the volume on the phone before entering. There was very little light coming through under the door. She didn't want it to go off and wake anyone.

The mild vibration in her hand startled her before she got the key in the door. Looking down it was a text from home.

We'll try to bug you less tomorrow.
Never doubt you are needed.
Have fun. I love you.

She smiled to herself. She had needed that text more than she knew until she got it. Maybe there was a way. She chuckled before going in; One small step for Margo...

Turning the key, she tried the cry on under her breath.

"Viva la Revolution!"

It felt good, really good.

My reply is no

Abi woke up disoriented. The television was on, so was the bathroom light. A soft snore came from the other bed, and someone was humming nearby. She assumed it was Dani when she saw the air mattress empty, but rounding the corner to where the sink and bathroom mirror were, it was Meredith.

"Are you one of those happy morning people?" she asked half-lidded.

Meredith grinned back at her in the mirror. "Why yes, yes I am. You're not?"

"Not until after coffee."

"Lucky for you Dani already left on a quest to acquire some."

"Oh thank gods, someone I can relate to." she managed to get out on a rough whisper. Abi noticed as Meredith buttoned up her blouse the same light colored under suit she'd noticed the day before in the car.

"Forgive me being incredibly rude, but you did say maybe later...how's now? What are you wearing?" she asked pointing to the last bit that was showing before Meredith buttoned over it.

Meredith hesitated for a moment before pronouncing plainly, "It's my garments."

"Should I know what that means?"

"Probably not. You're not Mormon. Think of it like my holy underwear."

Abi tried not to react other than matter of fact. "I didn't know you're Mormon."

Meredith laughed softly. "That probably depends on who you ask, but yes, I'm Mormon."

"Somehow I'm surprised. I guess part of me would think the church would frown on you being in Vegas."

"Why? Donnie & Marie are here." She quipped with a smile.

Abi's faux pas showed across her features back at her in the mirror. She covered them quickly. "Oh. Yeah, I guess they are aren't they?"

"I'm just teasing you, the church proper would be less than

pleased I'm sure."

"But here you are."

"Yes, here I am. Which goes back to if I'm a Mormon or not."

"You say that like you're unsure." Abi asked more than said.

"Not so much unsure as undecided."

"Well…" Abi tried to come up with a good response feeling completely out of her element on the subject, "I would think you have your reasons for that. What I know of you is that you are not one to act on a whim. You're very determined in your behaviors, and your comments most of the time I've noticed. This insight sheds new light on, and makes your reactions to Margo's comments yesterday about churches make a little more sense though."

"Margo knows the whole of the story and the struggle I'm having with what to do." Meredith frowned. "I was hoping we could suspend the subject for the weekend. I did. She didn't."

Abi put both hands up defensively. "I'm not prying or pushing. I just wondered what the fabric was. The only thing I was coming up with was like that jumpsuit thing that people wear when they work out so they sweat more and get more loss from water weight. If that was it, I was going to tear it from your body and burn it. I can already fit four of you in my thigh."

Meredith's mouth dropped open in shock. "You would not! And don't even go there. You so could not fit me in your thigh, not even one of me."

"Ha! I'll bet you my coffee that I can fit at least two."

"Can I just say I think I love you Abi?" Meredith said with a wide smile.

"Yes you can, but only because I tell it true, not because I have big thighs."

Meredith started laughing and dropped her toothbrush just as she was bringing it to her mouth. As they watched, it bounced off the corner of the counter and did a perfect backflip into the trashcan, splattering toothpaste across the mirror as it went. "Well crap!"

"Lucky for you I have a spare." Abi got out after the laughter died down.

The door opened around the corner then and the scent of coffee wafted into the room. Abi leaned out and hand called Dani to where they were still fighting fits of giggles at the spray of Crest on the mirror.

"You are a goddess!" she finally said when Dani handed her a cup.

"I'll take that over the 'blonde swimsuit lady' I got while waiting in line."

"Where did you get Starbucks?" Meredith asked looking at

the cups.

"It's a couple blocks down Freemont. There was a long line. Sorry if it's cold. I had to shake a couple followers on my way back. I hope the green tea latte is okay a little less than steaming hot."

"I wondered what was taking so long." Meredith replied, a concerned look on her face.

Abi took a long sip. Even tepid it was just the shot of go juice she needed, though she was quite awake after the toothbrush acrobatics. Hot would be better, but this was good and service in her pajamas was worth it. She hesitated her comment, but thought maybe for the next round or tomorrow it would be a good one anyway.

"You do know there's a coffee shop in the lobby right?"

"NO!" Dani wailed.

Abi grinned. "There's a coffee shop in the lobby if we need to go on a coffee run."

"SonOfA…" Dani groaned. "Now you tell me."

"If I had known you were going to be up at the butt-crack of dawn to go get coffee I might have mentioned it. It just hadn't come up yet. No worries. I'm sure we'll need more."

"Abi you're lucky you're cute." Dani mocked.

"She thinks I'm cuuute." Abi squealed in her best Rudolph with tar on his nose falsetto.

"What are you three on about now?" came from a gravelly

voice around the corner.

Abi ducked hard with a half grimace, half frown on her face. "Ooops. Sorry Margo."

"Nah, no sorry, I'm up. Did I smell coffee?"

Dani moved to take her a cup. Abi and Meredith followed behind dropping on the end of the bed in the dim.

"Time's a wastin, you two need to get moving so we can go." Dani said handing over the last cup of coffee to Margo but eyeing Abi.

A bit over an hour later they had picked up Raven and were seated at a diner. Abi couldn't help but notice that she was the only one having what she considered breakfast. The self-sabotage voice in her head didn't miss the chance to add that it was also part of why they looked like they did and she looked like she did.

Glancing around the table there was two eggs and toast, an oatmeal with fruit, a cheese omelet, and a poached egg with a melon wedge. In front of her was a stack of blueberry pancakes and bacon. She had caught a couple raised eyebrows at the order, but hadn't thought much about it. Seeing the stack now she was rethinking her choice. That they had essentially dumped blueberry pie filling over the pancakes was not helping the case at all.

She scraped the goop from the top of the stack and managed to eat some. Mostly she pushed cut up pieces around her plate. She finished the bacon and refilled her coffee.

"Aren't you hungry?" Raven asked watching her.

"They're not very good." Abi replied. Which really was true.

"You can order something else. We've got time."

"It's okay. I'm not going to wither away any time soon."

Meredith put her fork down. "I'm saying it now Abi. I don't want to hear any more of this kicking yourself about your size. You are not the big person you think you see in the mirror."

Abi was embarrassed to be called out at the table in front of the others. She appreciated what Meredith meant to do, it just stung a little out in the open. She did her best to deflect the comment.

"What did I say? I'm not going to wither away because I don't eat the pancakes. It's the truth, not a jab."

Raven headed the conversation off as Dani got up and left the table for the ladies room. "So what are you working on? Is it coming out soon that we can read it?"

Abi spluttered. "It is really hard. I have never written anything more than poetry or lyrics really so I don't know if I'm any good. Nobody reads or buys poetry. I want to be good. I'm trying to be. I think I'm more likely failing forward word by word."

"Well, you know you have a built in audience. We all love

to read." Raven countered with a smile.

"Ha! I know what you guys read…good stuff. I'm not there yet."

"Ha yourself. I'm sure we've all read our share of crap."

"Raven, you're a crazy good friend, but for how many of those 'shares' of crap, did you know the author and have to look them in the eye and LIE that you liked it?" Abi whined.

Raven smirked hard. "You never said anything about lying to you. I figured we'd just tell you it was crap."

Abi nearly forgot the pile of pancake mush in front of her, pulling back from dropping her forehead into it instead of the table top just in time. "Gee thanks Raven, real incentive there."

Raven shoved an elbow into Abi's forearm. "Calm down. I'm just kidding with you. That it means that much to you makes it so that no matter what, it's going to be better than you think. You actually are worried about sucking which is so much farther than a lot of writers out there ever got. Just do one thing for me, for us, and for yourself…don't forget this feeling. Don't forget how it feels to be a little bit scared to do poorly. Don't become THAT writer who is too full of themselves to know they really do suck. Okay?"

Abi looked up. Just past Raven was Meredith. She mouthed to her with a clenched fist, 'Viva la Revolution.' When Abi didn't immediately respond, she leaned in expectantly.

Abi relented. "Okay. I can do that much."

Don't count on it

Margo eyed the Magic 8-ball on the console as they piled back in. Would Dani know she had touched it? They had waited by the truck for a solid ten minutes for her to come back from her latest trip to the washroom.

"Everything come out all right?" She muttered as Dani fired up the engine.

"Yes it's fine. My stomach is sour."

"Really? I wonder why that would be. Let's see, oh I know…because you're empty."

"I just ate. I am not empty."

"Really? I'm willing to bet cash I don't have that you are."

"Damn it Margo, leave my insides out of this." Dani

huffed.

"Prove me wrong and I will."

"What, you want to go back and look at it? I'm sure it's gone. I flushed." Dani said through clenched teeth.

No one in the backseat was saying a word. In fact, each was making a concerted effort to watch something out the window, on the floor, or under their fingernails. Help was not coming from the backseat for either of the women up front.

"Look, I'm worried okay? I'm a nurse remember? I don't need you passing out or worse on us. We're in the middle of the damn desert."

"I am not going to pass out." Dani rolled her eyes.

"Says you Dani. I was in the room last night when your soup left. You were gone from breakfast three times. I think I have reason to worry."

"Oh my god. You won't stop will you?"

"Nope. I'm like a dog with a bone. And baby, I'm a pit-bull."

"I run on less than this most days. I ate breakfast. You saw me eat." Dani sneered.

"Yes, and I saw you leave. Did you heave it?"

"No."

"Should we ask Magic 8?"

"He doesn't work like that."

"You better not have heaved your breakfast. There wasn't

that much there to begin with. Your figure will survive the weekend." Margo said fishing in her bag. "Here, I grabbed a bottle of water on my way out. Drink."

"If it will shut you up I'll down the whole thing right here." Dani said reaching for the bottle.

"No, you need to drink a little bit over time." Margo pulled it back slightly to make her point.

"Who made you water god this morning?"

"You did." Margo stated as though it were fact.

"I did not. I would remember that."

"You did. Trust me. This is what I do. Oh, and we need to find an ATM." Margo added.

Dani put the truck in gear, likely leaving skid marks in the parking lot pulling out. The steam rising off the pavement didn't compare for the heat coming off her from the driver's seat. Small talk kicked up from the backseat as they drove, but it was low volume.

Abi and Raven were asking Meredith about her dating life and if she was getting out there. Meredith was hedging details but finally admitted to having met someone. Margo sat back and watched for banks as they drove. Her phone had not rung all morning. She was obviously trying not to check again for messages.

Finally, out near the edge of town, Margo spotted a bank with a drive up ATM that had enough room for her to get out and walk up.

"There's one. Pull in there." She directed loudly.

Dani obliged, pulling in perpendicular so Margo would not have far to walk, but could still have privacy to do her banking.

"Anyone else need to get cash while we're here?" she asked putting the vehicle in park.

Three heads shook negative from the backseat.

"Any objection to leaving Margo here?"

"We can't leave her here. She's just trying to watch out for you. It'll be okay." Raven said calmly.

"My own mother didn't think I needed one when I was growing up, I sure as hell don't need one now." Dani clipped out.

The three women from the backseat stared but didn't speak. Dani realized what she had said long after it was possible for it to be unspoken. "Sorry."

Abi opened her mouth to speak but Dani cut her off. "No. I don't want to talk about it." Abi closed her mouth as though she hadn't opened it.

Margo got back in the truck. "I'm good. What did I miss? Did my phone ring?"

Meredith spoke up then, "No your phone didn't ring. Do you need to check? I'm sure you're dying to."

Margo wanted to respond but lashed back instead, "Did

you notice there's a church right there? Don't you need a moment?"

Margo watched Meredith's fist ball up on her lap and put hers up in supplication. "I'm sorry. That was out of line…again."

"Yeah, it was." Meredith retorted.

"Okay…okay. Let's shut off the car and everyone get out and take five minutes." Raven said. "It's getting really hot in here and I'm not sure why, but we need to drop it down a notch."

Dani shut off the engine. All five women piled out and walked different ways away from the truck. Margo walked all of three steps before turning and heading toward Dani.

"I'm sorry I put you on the spot." She began before she reached her.

"You should be. That was embarrassing, and rude, and I don't even know what else to call that."

"I know. You have me scared and I run my mouth when I'm scared."

"Evidently you insult too."

"Yeah that too, with adults anyway. You can't do that with kids, it doesn't work." Margo lamented.

"Margo, I'm not a kid. I'm a grown woman who has managed to survive up to this point. Give me a break. Actually, maybe you should try giving yourself a break while you're at it. You've lashed out left and right since you got here."

"I know. And, I know you are. Please understand that I'm scared for you." Margo pleaded. "I heard you lose dinner last night. You put coffee on an empty stomach this morning, then you barely ate enough to run an infant and you were up from the table three times. I'm a damned nurse. It's what I do. Do you know how terrible I'd feel if you got sick on my watch?"

Dani shook her head. "Margo, I'm not…this is not your 'watch', you're off the clock. This is our 'Girl's weekend', remember?" she emphasized with finger quotes. "We're here to be reckless and wild. You have got to let us have room to do that. You can't control everything. It's not fun that way. Not for us, and I can't imagine for you either."

"So you're saying I'm screwing it up." Margo said with a frown.

"I'm saying, you don't have to be everybody's mom right now. You need to let go a little." Dani said gently.

"I don't know how."

"Yes you do. You just haven't for so long you're rusty."

Margo sighed. Dani was right. She had been the one in control and running every detail of everyone's life around her for so long that she was no longer one of any group, she was the master and commander of everything in the world around her. For as much as she wanted to fit in, she was doing a fine job of pushing everyone away.

"Can we take a couple more minutes? I need to talk to Meredith." She asked Dani before turning to walk away.

"As much as you need." Dani called after her.

When she reached Meredith, Meredith's face had changed to one of defense. "Did you come to give me more hard time?"

"No. I came to say I'm sorry." Margo said before closing the last few steps.

"I can't believe you did that to me. Two days in a row too. You know how hard I'm trying to figure this out and make a decision." Meredith challenged.

"Yes, I know how hard you're making it on yourself. I think you know your decision. I just want you to own it."

"Margo that isn't up to you." Meredith insisted.

"I know. I should have kept my mouth shut."

"Yes, you should have. Maybe I do know what my decision is. Maybe I don't. You don't understand. Your kids do exactly what you want all the time. They're still young. You tell them to jump and they keep jumping until you say stop. Jamie I tell to slow down and she runs faster. How can I decide to leave a path she is intent to pursue? How can I be there to guide her if I'm no longer welcome?" Meredith gushed out in a long wave of run together words.

"Maybe that's a question for Abi or Raven, their kids are older. I think you know the answer though. I can't tell you, and really neither can they." Margo said. "But somewhere soon you have to do more than just know, you have to do."

"I know. What I know too is that I really need you to knock it off about the churches. You're killing me Margo."

"Okay. I'll stop. I'm stepping in it left and right it seems. I gotta do something right for a change. No more churches comments this weekend…deal?"

"Deal. You might want to lay off Dani's eating habits too." Meredith added. "I've never seen her get so steamed and she's been given chances left and right since we arrived."

"Yeah, I got that too. But if she doesn't eat something more before we go out tonight, I'm going to be crawling out of my skin to watch her drink." Margo sighed.

"She doesn't need a mother. She needs a friend. We all do. You think you might be up for the job?" Meredith tried to redirect gently.

"I want to be."

"Don't 'want' to be…be."

Margo snorted. "Last night it's some revolutionary, today it's Jedi Master…what a trip this is turning out to be."

"That's MS. Jedi Master to you young lady. I am still your elder." Meredith ribbed with her finger wagging.

"Uh-huh. Sure, sure. Whatever you say there Yoda." Margo

laughed.

Yes definitely

As they pulled into a parking lot in front of what appeared to be a large old mining shed, Abi watched a rollercoaster wind in and out of the building. Curbside, heading toward the lot was a group of men in Marine uniforms carrying instruments.

"Damn, we missed the band." She commented wistfully.

Meredith turned to see what Abi was staring at, giving a long slow whistle. "Mmmm, you have got, got, got to love a man in uniform."

Abi giggled. "Shake the 8-ball Dani quickly." She said tapping incessantly at Dani's shoulder in the front. "Quicker than that…shake it NOW!"

"Okay, okay…but what's the question?" Dani said reaching for the black orb.

"I'll ask the question, just shake it and nobody move until it answers." Abi said excitedly.

She composed herself and watched Dani get a good shake in before asking her question. "Magic 8, should we sit here for just a moment and ogle the Marines?"

Raven, Meredith, and Margo busted out laughing. Dani looked back at her in the rearview mirror shaking her head. "Really? That's the question? Don't think you could have decided that on your own?"

"Well, it seems to me that my directing it to be, and Magic 8 saying we should, have two different possible results and I know what I would want to do, but you know…" Abi grinned.

Margo snorted. "Oh yes, because you're the only hot blooded woman in the car who wants to stare at the Marines and needed a reason to do it."

"Short of sunglasses, the tinted windows really do afford us a longer look you know. It would have been kind of rude to get out and openly stare don't you think?" Abi rationalized.

Raven was chuckling under her breath as she spoke. "Of course Abi, because openly staring from behind tinted glass is so much less skeevy."

As the group of men passed beyond them and they got a look at them walking away, there were several contented sighs. Abi was too busy watching to notice who else was appreciating her Magic 8 question, or the answer that afforded the opportunity. She couldn't be sure but she thought it was Meredith whose quiet, "Very nice" was met with several 'mmm-hmm' responses.

The ignition was finally clicked off and they piled out. Abi took several glances backwards as they walked toward the building earning her a shoulder swat from Meredith. "Didn't have quite enough of a look?"

"Guess not." Abi grinned with a loose shrug.

As they entered there was a little gift shop and a large casino area. It was in fact an old mining facility as suspected from the parking lot, and the roller coaster did in fact weave in and out of the building. Abi couldn't help but wonder what they did when it rained. In the middle of the desert maybe that didn't really matter.

They wandered through the casino area and found the restrooms first, regrouping after every one had freshened up. The counter for the coaster was empty in the distance. Abi was more than a little surprised by this. The Desperado was legendary. How could there be no line? The oldest operating wooden roller coaster in the US, it should be slammed with people waiting to ride. She thought.

"Looks like we could each have our own car." She said vacantly as she watched the coaster slice through above the casino.

"I know, that's so odd." Meredith chirped. "I call front seat."

"Guess we'll have to ride twice. I like the front car." Abi replied.

"You guys fight over it, I'll be at the slots" Margo added.

Before she thought, Abi retorted "Don't you like roller coasters?"

Margo held up her leg firmly encased in the boot. "The insurance is already giving me fits for a second surgery this year if this boot doesn't work and they have to pin it. I don't need to give them a reason to deny me by worsening the damage. I don't think there's any justification for roller coaster that they'd buy."

"I'm so sorry. I forgot for a minute." Abi replied.

Margo shrugged. "It's okay. I want to pull at least a couple arms at a machine while we're here. Can't win if I don't play."

"Ha!" Abi retorted. "I am the opposite. Can't lose if you don't play."

"Glass half empty eh?" Margo asked quizzically.

"Nah, realist through and through."

"Your toe is mighty close to crossing that line you've drawn there." Margo added as she walked away and the others moved to get tickets. Abi didn't respond, but couldn't help but wonder to herself if she was in fact dancing perilously close to being or becoming a pessimist.

When they reached the counter, the reason for the lack of patrons, or at least one possible reason appeared. It was $15.00 for a single ride. For that price, it made sense at least to Abi why there was no line.

"I don't know about anyone else, but I'm thinking one ride will be enough for me at this rate." She said.

Meredith was nodding. "I agree. You can have the front

car. I'm used to the second or third one anyway."

"No ma'am." Abi retorted. "We can share the front car, or you can have it. You called it first."

Meredith gave her a stunning grin. "Let's share. We can both have it."

"That works for me."

Four tickets were stamped and collected before they made their way up to the loading platform, giggling like they were kids the whole way. Abi and Meredith climbed into the front car with Raven and Dani in the second seat. There was no one else riding.

True to claims, it was a fast ride. More than once along the way Abi had to remember to shut her mouth so she wouldn't lose her gum. No one in the second seat was going to thank her for getting that in their hair at high speed. Weaving in and out of the building she looked for Margo below but never spotted her.

She turned at one point to grin at Meredith as they climbed for a new descent. She bit her tongue and looked back to the front at seeing a tear weeping back toward Meredith's ear. Wind, joy, or some other emotion she wasn't going to guess, but the accompanying expression suggested it was due to something miles away from sadness.

Abi spit her gum into her hand before the next drop and screamed the entire rest of the ride. There was something inside that she didn't want to inspect too closely that needed out. No one would know the hard emotions she put into the scream and let fly on the wind. They weren't quite in Vegas, but these things could and should stay here. It was high time to liberate herself from the chains.

Very doubtful

Dani immensely enjoyed going to rescue Margo from her stilted cycle of deposit coins, pull the lever, cuss, and deposit more coins. They had piled back into the vehicle and headed the short distance to the outlet mall. Meredith and Abi had been notably quiet since the ride, but everyone seemed ready for some serious shopping as they piled out.

Walking up to the nearest store to enter, a man walking out caught Dani's eye. It took her a minute to place him, but he was one of the guys from a recent episode, or maybe re-run of Last Comic Standing. She made a beeline for him.

"Hey. You're a comedian right?" she began.

"Yeah, and?" They guy was obviously not familiar with greeting fans or being noticed.

"I caught your act. My boyfriend thinks you're the next big deal. He'll never believe this. Can I get a picture with you?" She gushed.

The look on his face said he wasn't buying her comments as genuine. He acquiesced anyway with a shrug of one shoulder. "Sure."

They posed together and Raven snapped a couple quick pictures before they were moving again. Not however, until one last exchange. "Can I get your autograph too? Michael is never going to believe this." Dani said while fishing for a scrap of anything to write on. Abi pulled her breakfast receipt out and handed it to her with a pen. "Here."

The guy smirked at the slip of paper but was a good sport. "Sure, you're kinda cute, anything for a fan. Save that…it might be worth something someday." He said as he handed it back.

"I'm counting on it." Dani smiled back as he handed her the pen back too.

After he walked off into the parking lot the conversation caught up to Dani. She turned to the group with a look of shock on her face. "Did he seriously just say I was 'kinda cute'?"

"What's wrong with that?" Abi questioned.

"I don't think I've been 'kinda cute' since I was ten." Dani replied plainly. "I don't think he knew at all who I was."

Margo rolled her eyes. "So? He didn't know who any of the rest of us were either."

"No, no…that's a weird, I mean good thing. Unusual, but good I think." Dani wondered openly as she responded. "I wasn't trying to sound conceited, it was…nice." Her tone was one of shock.

"Okay then, are we shopping?" Margo said moving toward the doors.

They made their way around the different outlet shops. Dani noticed that Abi was walking the rows with a fierce look of determination on her face that faltered to disappointed again and again. She herself had found rack after rack of things she would love to get, but made a mental note to stop on the way home, not whip out her card for a spending spree just now. She waited until Abi was several aisles away from the group before wandering over, trying to appear casual.

"Find anything?" she opened.

Abi shrugged. "Not really. Lots of cute, but nothing I can wear."

Abi had poked at and mocked herself from arrival. Dani had never really stopped to look at her beyond the person she knew. The idea that she could not shop in this store was never a thought as the others were all finding things. Abi was not big by any equation, but she was not small. Being dressed by others for so long, Dani really never considered sizes anymore, so she had no idea how to gauge why Abi couldn't shop here, just her statement that she couldn't.

Dani became determined to find something that could work and began quizzing Abi. "How much room to you have in your luggage?"

"What?" Abi replied startled.

"Room...space? You know, to take stuff home...I mean we can't shop without knowing if you can actually get it home right? Or, you might have to be indentured to me to ship it to you if you can't transport it. I just never know when I might need an assistant of some kind." Dani was mocking trying to lighten the look on Abi's face. If she realized the ploy or not, Abi went with it, a confused grin finally coming to the surface.

"I don't have a lot of room if that's what you mean. I already filled some of it with the stuff for the family." Abi said as she followed Dani to the other side of the store.

"Did you get anything for yourself?" Dani asked back over her shoulder.

"No, not yet."

"Then we have a mission. And you, might have to do some creative packing to get it home. I can teach you."

Abi snorted hard from behind her, stopping Dani mid-step. She pivoted to face Abi who almost ran into her. "What was funny? I was serious."

"Dani, you arrived for a girl's weekend with two suitcases, an air mattress, and another carryon type bag complete with a Magic 8-ball for decisions. I'm not sure creative packing is your forte." Abi snickered out.

Dani got down in her face to whisper. "Abi, just because I didn't have to for this trip, doesn't mean I can't. Now don't blow my cover, it will be our secret that I'm more than just a 'kinda cute' thing."

Abi finger-crooked her to come back closer to her face as

Dani was standing back up. She waited for her to get close enough to whisper back. "Dani, if you ever again tell me that it's a secret that you are more than your looks, I'm going to kick you in the knees. I knew that before I ever saw your face."

"I can do that, but I have one in return, and it will be your ass I'll be kicking not your knees." Dani looked at her sternly before continuing. "I don't want to hear another word about you being anything or nothing because of your dress size, and that means down face too. I did not choose to meet you, or call you friend…any of you" she waved her arm around in the air, "because of how anyone did or didn't look. You guys got to know me, not my looks, or shape, and that's just one of those things that I don't get from most people. Return the good juju…love yourself that much too."

Dani noticed a tear streak Abi's face. "Ohhh no, knock that shit off right now. No tears. We don't know each other's roads, but we get to walk this one together by choice…I don't need wet socks now."

"Dani you are such a freak show. Wet socks? Really? You make me feel like I kind of fit in with someone like you and you're worried about wet socks?"

"No I'm not worried about wet socks you dolt, I'm worried

about you making me cry too and then we'll have a scene in the outlet mall." Dani shook her head and rolled her eyes at Abi. "And for the record, I know more than most people think about what it takes to fit in, you'll always fit with me."

"I'm sorry. I just feel a bit like Abbott and Costello standing near you. I'm not insecure, but then again…I am."

Dani snorted hard before toning it down as several nearby shoppers looked up. She dropped back to hushed tones. "Abi, I'm insecure every day, and for reasons that you'd never guess. I'm insecure standing next to you…you're a freaking author and…"

"Aspiring." Abi corrected.

"Whatever Abi, you're trying. And I hate that word by the way. Aspiring…pffft. You're putting one word after another which makes you an author to me. I'm just another freaking pretty face to most of the world who never stop to wonder if I have an active brain cell in my head. I would bet my left nut, which I don't have by the way, that most people would be stunned that I CAN read never mind that I met some of the best friends I have ever had, online in conversation threads, having discussions about what we have read.

People may look at you and think you're 'kinda cute' but

they don't say so, they don't need to. They say other things like how smart you are, or talented, or that you have beautiful children. I don't get any of that. I'm the girl on the magazine, the model, or 'kinda cute'. There isn't an effort to know more, it's as if all I am is my looks."

"But Dani you're not." Abi said aghast.

Dani cut her off. "And neither are you." She put her finger in Abi's face to make the point.

Abi stared back at her. Whatever she was thinking, she wasn't saying. Dani watched her face as several things crossed and rearranged themselves before she spoke her simple response.

"Thanks Dani."

Dani realized she had said a lot more than she planned to say and once again, couldn't take any of it back. She would have back pedaled if she could have, but it was out now and by the look on Abi's face, she had heard and processed every word. What was it about Abi that made her speak first and think later she wondered? The best she could do was try to detour now and hope that it would fade to backdrop before long.

"Now, come with me…they have a killer pair of stilettos

that would be amazing with just about anything, and I happen to know there is a lingerie shop on the other side of the mall that I'm sure we can find something in. Hubs will never know what hit him if you pull that out of the gift bag when you get home."

Abi's face faltered. Dani knew she had successfully detoured as Abi's squeaked out, "Lingerie?"

Cannot predict now

It was getting late. They had decided to hit one last store on their way out before going to get ready for their big night out on the town. Margo noticed Dani's look of longing before the hard wall slammed down as they entered. They'd walked smack into the middle of the baby section.

She had never stopped to enquire, but hesitated just a moment in her thoughts now. Dani never talked about kids. In fact, when the conversation was kids, Dani always seemed to be otherwise busy. Even yesterday passing pictures around, Dani had moved from the room to hang clothes up while she, Abi & Meredith had been talking about and sharing snaps of their respective offspring and families.

Margo did more than wonder, but kept it to herself as Dani maneuvered them through the department to accessories before anyone else so much as noticed her face. She thought to herself that she surely must have been mistaken. Dani had never said a thing one way or the other. It must have been something else she had noticed as they walked in that caused the change in facial expressions.

Dani was tall, blonde, and beautiful. She had a handsome boyfriend and they lived a fast lifestyle. Kids did not fit in that picture at all. She discarded the idea completely.

Meredith and Raven were looking at handbags. Dani and Abi had moved to stockings, which was amusing in a way since they had spent over an hour in a lingerie store just two stops before. Margo moved to the racks of shoes and boots. Everything here was marked way down and she couldn't help herself, she was dying to try some on. She was going to have to settle for staring at them instead.

It was a rare treat that she bought anything for herself, never mind something like shoes or boots that would be anything more than functional. She seldom dressed up anymore. They were always on the move somewhere and it was hardly practical to have anything more than tennis shoes or flats on.

She mentally chided herself that it would have been fun trying them on, but there was no point to getting attached to any so why bother? Given her current state, she wouldn't be able to wear them any time soon and they would be out of fashion long before then anyway. With a hard sigh she sat on a bench in the middle of the row and looked longingly at box after box of cute, really cute, Cinderella at the ball gorgeous shoes across from her.

She stared down at the boot and wondered what it would be like to get to wear cute shoes. She was not proud of the venomous thought as she noticed Dani's designer sandals through the rack in the aisle on the other side. They all had their cross to bear right? Dani must have one somewhere, though for the life of her she couldn't spot it.

She thought more on the face she had seen Dani make as they had come in. Was it really all in her mind or was there something there? Margo had made a life out of reading peoples expressions of pain and longing when they were sick, was she over thinking it now, or did she miss a chance to be a better friend?

As she sat and thought it through, she kicked herself again that she hadn't said something. She wasn't sure how, or what to say. She did want to be a better friend. She felt like she needed to try to make up the lost ground and find a way to fit in. It was high time to use her powers for good.

It had been drilled into her in her medical training that mental health was a large part of physical health. Was she healthy, she wondered? For all the breaks and near breaks, she would say no.

Raven plopped down on the bench beside her, jarring her from her thoughts making her jump. "You going to try some on or just stare at them?"

"What's the point?" Margo muttered.

"The point, is that they could be something to work for."

"Or they could be something to let me down later. I have no idea what this leg is going to look like or what will fit after this heals, or surgery if it comes to that." Margo sulked.

"Yeah. You're right about that. But, at these prices wouldn't it be worth the risk?" Raven asked softly. "Are you the pessimist you asked Abi about earlier? Who knows? Maybe they'll be perfect. You seem like you need something to boost your spirits. You've been down and kind of biting today. That's really not the person I think I got to know."

"Raven, I'm just so tired. No, that's not quite right. I'm tired of being tired is probably a better way to say it. I'm broken and exhausted."

"You're not broken, though your spirit sure seems intent to be. I get the tired part. I raised my daughter and now I have a grandchild in my home. I'm tired before I get up. I can't hear the baby cry and not react, even from a sound sleep. I understand tired. But, I also understand joy, and I wouldn't trade what I have right now. Would you?"

"Not trading or settling for less is why I'm in this boot. It isn't that I would trade it, I just would like to not feel like I'm always running behind it. I want to be doing it with everyone, not watching as it happens because I can't participate. Being benched to the sidelines is as bad as not being there at all." Margo nearly sobbed.

"But you are there. As best as you can, you are there." Raven admonished. "There is no question that you are there."

"My mom never was. I can't do that to my kids and I feel like I am. All the time I feel like my kids look up and I'm not there, I'm sitting somewhere else because I can't be where they are. In my mind it's the same."

"Margo, it's not the same, not even close." Raven chastised.

"Then why does it feel like it?" Margo asked quietly.

Raven snorted. "Because you are ridiculously stubborn and hard on yourself? Because you are so far bent trying not to be your mother that it has become the only point of reference in your mind? Because you've run yourself so far down that you can't recover before you knock yourself back again? Take your pick. You my friend, are your own worst enemy and the reason why you can't recover. You aren't allowing yourself to see the scene where you are happy, healthy, and in the picture too."

"And the solution Dr. Whitley?" Margo mocked.

"Buy the shoes." Raven chuckled back. "You need something to work for that doesn't have anything to do with your kids, your mother, or your health. You need a goal that is just for you, so you can be a better you for everyone else."

"I haven't tried any on. I couldn't bring myself to see them not fit this mangled foot and ankle."

"What size should you be?"

"9 ½."

"Sit there, we've got work to do." Raven retorted as she moved to the racks in the right size and started pulling boxes down.

Margo watched in stunned disbelief at the choices Raven was bringing her. One pair she tried to push to the bottom of the stack thinking there was no way she'd wear them with the scars she was sure to have after this was all said and done. Raven caught her shuffling the box to the bottom.

"Oh no missy, those first. No disregarding my choices before you even get the boot off and try." Raven scolded before walking away to grab more.

Margo gingerly removed the boot. She stared at the shoes in the box for a long while before reaching down and putting the one on her good foot first. It was pretty. Without letting herself feel too Disney, she thought it was a bit fairytale looking. She'd never been a princess. Her injuries and constant running had always been her evil adversary.

Raven returned with several pair of low heeled boots. "Hey, that looks good." She said as she put the boxes down. "Let's see them both on."

Margo grimaced before moving to put the other one on. She wanted to see it on. She also didn't want to see it on. Her leg was less than pretty with its shades of yellow fading bruise. It was also slightly swollen even after time because she hadn't stayed off of it as she'd been told to. She mentally finally acknowledged the truth that she had refused to voice. She was her own worst enemy and the obstacle she could never seem to overcome.

She slipped the shoe on. It hurt. It was not going to be something she could wear. A tear slipped down her face at the reality more than the physical pain. When Raven came up with several new offerings, she brushed it away before it could become an issue. "This one hurts a little."

"Then take it off silly. This is supposed to be fun. No tears."

They went through more than a dozen pair of shoes before they switched to boots. The boots didn't necessarily fit any better on the bum leg, but they looked better, and hid the vivid reminders of what she was doing to herself. Meredith walked up then, looking to Raven who was admiring the boots from another angle.

"You ditched me." Meredith said to Raven. "One minute we were in change purses and the next I was holding a bag talking to some guy holding his wife's purse."

Raven chuckled. "Oh no. I would have come back. Did you find anything?"

"No. Everything seems to be pretty themed over there and not themes I'm wearing any time soon."

"Then stay over here with us and let's do shoes." Raven replied with gusto.

Margo added, "Somebody should get cute shoes right. What size do you need? Raven has me squared in, she can pull for you too since I think the whole rack has been pulled for me already."

Raven stuck her tongue out at Margo. "You just keep trying them on, there's a pair here for you, and I can feel it." She turned to Meredith. "What size do you need?"

Meredith flagged her hands back and forth negative. "I have no room for shoes in my luggage. Don't even tempt me to look." She turned and walked away, commenting over her shoulder, "I'll see what the other two are up to."

Raven turned back to Margo, hip cocked out, foot tapping. "They aren't going to jump out of the box and try themselves on you know."

"Raven I know you mean well, but honestly don't you think this is futile? We have no idea what I am going to be able to wear later."

"Now you listen to me Margo Upton, I met this incredible, compassionate, hard working woman on line who doesn't seem to take 'no' for an answer from anyone for anything. She doesn't let things slow her down even when they are things that SHOULD slow her down. Imagine my surprise when I meet her live and find that she is kicking herself over and over again so she does not become something she isn't?

You have the gun loaded and have the trigger cocked for what may be once this is all done. Have a little faith in yourself to overcome it, and believe in yourself that you can. You are never going to be more than this if you stop trying. And, you are never going to be everything you are trying so hard to reach if you don't heal. Get out of your own way."

Margo reached for another boot. Raven was right. There was no way anything would be different the way she was doing things. She thought to herself, *what's the saying?* If you always do what you've always done, you'll always get what you've always gotten. She was tired of being broken.

It was high time to trade up. Even if it was boots, she was getting something to trade for. Today.

Outlook good

Meredith stared out the window as they made their way back to Vegas. She was half listening to Raven and Margo chatting about the boots they had found and how goals were important but achieving them was more important than having them. She had goals. No one seemed to be interested in her goals though.

Abi nudged her shoulder from the center seat. "You lost in a daydream or can anyone take the trip?"

"Just thinking. You?"

Abi shrugged. "Wondering what the night will bring. I

loved the roller coaster though. I wish it hadn't been so expensive to ride."

"Yeah, but it was fun to be in front for a change."

Abi canted her head to the side. "You never ride in front do you?"

"When I drive."

"I think I could get used to be chauffeured." Abi said with a smile making a show of kicking back against the headrest and stretching her legs out.

Meredith chuckled. "I never think about it like that. I always feel like I'm the grownup still stuck at the kids table for Christmas, like I'm not quite arrived or big enough to move up."

"Maybe that's because none of the rest of us fit at the kids table." Abi said jokingly.

Dani paused her 'Nnn-cha' bouncing to interject. "Abi we made a deal."

"I was commenting on Meredith being maybe a size zero if she stuffed a parka under her shirt, not on my size. Calm down." Abi replied to the glaring eyes in the rearview mirror.

Meredith turned to Abi with her eyes wide. "I am not a size zero thank you very much."

"I was kidding Meredith."

"You better be." Meredith said. "I wasn't talking about my size anyway. I feel like no one sees me, or if they do, they don't see that I'm worth their time or attention."

"You're worth my time and attention." Abi said unequivocally.

"That's not what I mean."

"Okay, so help me understand." Abi said quietly.

Meredith looked around the car at the others. Dani had resumed her bouncing and Raven and Margo were talking about ways to strengthen Margo's leg to get into the new boots they had found together. Satisfied that she was not the center of everyone's attention for this, she leaned back and rolled her head against the headrest to look at Abi, speaking quietly.

"I was raised in the church. I was married to the church before I was married to Mark, and in both relationships I've always felt like I was somehow a second class citizen. I thought after the divorce that I would feel differently, but I don't. I have been debating for a long time leaving the church too because I don't feel like I fit there anymore either."

"So, what's holding you back? It seems to me you have reasons for wanting to leave, why don't you?"

"Because Jamie is getting ready to go through her endowment and I can't support her in that if I'm no longer welcome."

"Why wouldn't you be welcome? And, since I missed class on the day they talked about it, what's endowment besides cleavage?" Abi asked.

Meredith let out a loud bark of laughter. "Ohmygoodnes. Endowment is at the conclusion of your religious teaching when you get your garments."

"The underwear? You have to go to class to get your underwear?" Abi asked, obviously stunned.

"Yeah. You go to class and then you get your *garments*." She emphasized the word so Abi would understand it was not just underwear. "If I leave the church, then I'm no longer part of that and I can't be there for her as she does it." Meredith replied. "It's like I don't fit in, but I can't fit out either."

Abi looked at her for a spell, obviously weighing how to ask the next question. Meredith waited, but when no comment came, as it was obvious there was one on the tip of Abi's tongue, she closed her eyes and spoke first. "Just say it."

"No, it's not a 'just say it' thing. I'm trying to figure out how it works. If you are wanting to leave the church, would Jamie stay? And, you are her mother, shouldn't that give you the right regardless of if she stays and you don't?"

Meredith was trying to think. The church was hard to explain to one who didn't understand it. She tried for an analogy.

"Do your daughters write?"

"Huh?" Abi was obviously taken off guard with the question.

"You are a writer, are you not?"

"I'm trying to be. But what does that have to do..."

"Go with me on this for a minute." Meredith asked calmly cutting her off.

"You are a writer, yes?"

"Yes."

"If the day came that you no longer wanted to be a writer

but one of your daughters did, would you still be able to help them be a writer?"

"Yes. I could."

"If there was some rule that said even though you know how to be a writer, you can't help because you no longer are a writer, would that be a problem?"

"I think I would be in someone's face about it, but no one is saying that to me. Neither of my girls want to write anyway." Abi cut to the chase she thought was coming.

"That's not what I mean, and it's where this is different. The church has rules. If I leave, I cannot be part of Jamie's endowment, even though I know how. And, Jamie wants to pursue this. I don't want her to, but I can't say so because it isn't my place to tell her that. That, and her dad is pushing her to do it, so it makes it me against them which means if I leave the church, I lose on both fronts."

Abi's eyes were wide and her mouth was doing the 'Oh' without sound. She regained her composure before she spoke.

"So you are saying Jamie is doing it period. It isn't an if you leave or stay question, she is going forward regardless. It is an if you leave the church, you are doing so knowing you also can't be a part of that for her."

"Yes."

"And it's the church's rule, not because you wouldn't be there from the outside if you could." Abi continued out loud.

"Yes."

Abi's hand came up and she drummed her fingers against her top lip for a spell before speaking again. The action was making Meredith antsy to know what she was thinking, but she waited impatiently for Abi to process it this time.

"I don't mean to sound indelicate Meredith, but do you have to be part of the church to support her? I mean really? I understand that you can't be part of the doctrine and dogma side of it, but is being there for her about that anyway?"

Meredith had opened her mouth to respond midway through Abi's questions. By the end she found she had to close her mouth and think about what to say. The answer had always been from the church's perspective and a glaring 'yes'. Abi's un-indoctrinated question might be the answer she had never been able to see. She was startled to be thinking about it and had to stall.

"Say that again."

"Maybe it's just me Meredith, but I'm not sure I understand. Why you have to be part of the church to show her the path she is trying to take if you know it? Is the hesitation about being part of the ceremony, or does somehow not being a part of the ceremony prevent you from being there to help her walk the path she is choosing, even if you disagree or no longer choose to walk that same path yourself?" Abi asked again, adding a new twist at the end.

"To me it sounds like the implication is somehow that you are not an aware enough or mature enough person to support someone whose goals in life are different than yours. That is not the person I know. Surely you can't believe that."

Meredith felt the load lift and the lightbulb click on. She had been looking at the situation all along from the perspective of how the church would view the decision, not what the implication of the decision was for her and Jamie. The decision to leave was easy, except for Jamie's choice to stay.

She had discarded the truth in lieu of the teachings that had been drilled into her. It had bogged her down for months trying to find a way to be okay with staying. She had told herself repeatedly it would be for Jamie and that she could fall on her training and habits to get her through for her daughter. She had made herself the second class citizen that she was trying to get rid of.

They pulled up at the Venetian to drop Raven off. Margo asked if Dani would wait a minute so she could run in to the powder room grabbing her right side as she reached for the door lever.

"That's a weird spot, sure it's not your appendix?" Dani asked.

"It's not. That came out last year." Margo replied matter of fact as she grabbed the handle to open the door.

"Just the same, I'll go with you. Anybody else?" Dani asked the back seat.

Abi and Meredith both shook their heads no as the others got out and went in.

Meredith was still reeling from the realization of the conversation they had been having. She turned to Abi before speaking. "Do you know how long I've been wrestling with this?"

Abi grinned wide. "Guess you should have told me sooner. I could have saved you so much grief."

Meredith rolled her eyes. "Funny girl aren't you? I'm

serious. I've been making myself sick about this for months. I don't want to be the bad guy in this situation and the only answer seemed to be to stay in the church. I don't want to stay in the church. I want to be worthy enough without the church."

"Meredith…" Abi started with her head canted, speaking softly. "Sweetie don't you know your worth has nothing to do with the church? Your worth is about you. Being a mom…good or bad, is about you. Showing your daughter the path she should be on, parenting in general…is hard as hell because they don't choose to walk the road you've paved. That's why we all have grey hair.

That you know the path she is choosing, or choosing to try, I think makes you one up on the rest of us. Most of us have no idea what our kids are trying to do, never mind how to guide them to get there. You CAN do this. You have to do it the best you are able though. It sounds to me like you know which way that is. Are you strong enough to do it is the only question that remains."

Meredith was overwhelmed by how easy it seemed as Abi said it out loud. "I'm going to need some serious help."

Abi giggled. "Lucky for you we have your back on this." Abi balled her fist and mocked popping it in the air. "Viva

Zapata?" she said more as a question than a statement.

Meredith grinned back, balling her own fist. Noticing Dani and Margo headed their way, she nodded quickly and gave her response to the person who had helped her find the path.

"Viva la Revolution!"

Reply hazy, try again

Abi and Meredith walked arm in arm down the hall to their room. The ride from the Venetian had been mostly traded grins in the backseat. The front seats had been an ongoing conversation about diet and internal functions. Margo had reminded Dani more than once on the ride that she needed to eat something before they went out. Abi had pursed her lips at Margo's 'white on rice' threat about harassing Dani if she didn't. Abi fought not to laugh as Margo was anything but white.

Reaching the room, everyone peeled off and started getting things ready for another evening out. Abi jumped up first.

"I'm going to get a shower, anyone need the bathroom?"

"I'll take one after we get back, there's no way my hair will be dry enough to crimp if I wash it now." Dani responded.

"No, you go ahead." Meredith and Margo replied together. They then shouted 'Jinx' together too which prompted Margo to jump up shouting "Double jinx, buy me a coke, no take backs."

Dani looked from Margo to Meredith then to Abi. "Well there's one I haven't heard."

"Come and visit my house, you'll hear it at least once a day from someone." Margo said laughing.

"Oh." Was Dani's response as she went back to getting clothes out for the evening.

Abi ducked into the bathroom. Back home, there was seldom enough hot water left by the time it was her turn to get a shower. The perks of being at a hotel, unlimited supply. She cranked the lever to scalding and pulled the curtain. She took a leisurely time soaping up and washing her hair.

It had been an enlightening, emotional, and educational day. It had been fun too. She felt like she'd made a connection with Dani and Meredith that hadn't been there before. Coupled with Margo's confession in the wee hours before sleep, it was adding up to be a great trip after all.

She regretted emerging from the spray but figured it would be nice if someone else got a shower if they wanted one. She wrapped up in a towel and tied her head in a hand towel as best she could before moving out to the main room. Her hot water high dropped with the air conditioned, empty room.

She walked to the door and peeked through the eye hole. No one was in the hall that she could see. She walked back toward the bathroom. No note, no nothing.

She sat on the end of the bed where she'd slept and looked at herself in the mirror over the long dresser sighing. Her inner monologue was not kind. In the reflection she saw every nuance of it as it echoed in her head. It was ugly.

She forced herself not to cave, not to cry, and not to give in to the overwhelming sense of being alone. She couldn't fathom where they would have gone, or why they didn't say anything at least through the bathroom door. They could have scribbled a note at the bare minimum. There was a little pad and pen on the nightstand.

Sure, none of them knew the self-sabotage she committed against herself in her heart every day, but she thought they had seen her insecurities. Maybe they didn't watch her as much as she watched them. Maybe they didn't catch the little things like she did. She still thought somehow they saw her.

As she stared at herself in the mirror, she knew she was wrong. Wrong about them seeing her, but also wrong about them deserting her. She tried to tell herself that they hadn't ditched her, she knew they hadn't. She couldn't shake the ache of it just the same. Old demons die hard, and seldom without a drawn out kicking, screaming, and biting match.

She had become so used to, and numbed out by the day to day life of being overlooked and undervalued that she couldn't quite bring herself to give people the benefit of the doubt at the little things. She knew this was the truth. It was a hard pill to swallow.

She yearned for someone to see her, really see her and value her. She thought Dani had, but maybe that was the element they were in at the time. She just wanted to be seen, just once as someone who needed. She didn't want to be needy, even though she was. Heck, they all were in some way. She wanted people to just know the way that she needed without having to expose her weakness and show it.

As she looked at herself thinking it, she was repulsed by it. She had worked a thankless job for years because it put food on the table and a roof over her family's heads. Not because she wanted to, because she had to. She had given up getting anything more years ago.

The realization that she had quit soured her stomach. She had been driven and resourceful once upon a time. Becoming a writer was her quiet struggle to reclaim what she felt was lost. It was a fire burning deep to make a name for herself that she could say with pride. "Ha!" she mocked her reflection. "Pride my ass. You can't even tell people you're a writer without hedging every other word."

Abi hung her head. She was a fraud. She was just another washed up wanna-be who had settled for becoming every woman. She had the requisite husband, two children, job, two cars complete with payments and a mortgage that was always an exercise in delicate budgeting to manage.

No matter how long she had waited for things to change, it never did. It always seemed like she was impatiently watching for the other shoe to drop. How great the irony that it dropped a thousand miles from home in Sin City sitting alone in a hotel room?

Back home the elusive drop always seemed a tick away. Back home, the shoe actually never dropped. She told herself she was too smart for that. Since she usually learned the lesson the first time, there wasn't usually a second shoe coming. Instead, it was the first one of a new pair that clobbered her when she wasn't looking or ready. She certainly hadn't seen this one coming.

Staring in the mirror she looked back over time at her life. She couldn't figure out when it had become such a parade of knock outs or why she had let it. It had been forever that she had been doing creative math to make the budget work and keep the household afloat. She had spent years she couldn't remember enough to count, repurposing things or hitting resale shops to keep up with growing kids and threadbare clothes.

Eons flashed back in the mirror at her of being last in line for dreams long forgotten. She wouldn't necessarily trade the time for what she had gotten in return, she just couldn't remember how she got to where she was. It had been ten thousand little things all happening over time when she wasn't watching. She watched them all now mock her from the mirror as she aged a little in the span of an hour.

For a long time she had blamed the economy. It was easy to do, everyone else certainly was. In her heart of hearts, if she was honest with herself, she knew that wasn't the whole truth. The grass was always greener on the side with the most manure her dad had always said. How she had longed for manure in her life on more than one occasion.

"Tell that to the girl in the mirror Pop." Came out unchecked just as she heard laughter in the hall beyond the door. Abi looked hard at herself in the mirror one last time as she heard the key and pasted a smile on her face as the door opened.

"Great gobs of goose shit y'all. I thought you had deserted me." She announced as her friends came in trying again to hide the truth behind humor.

Margo was in the lead carrying two pizza boxes.

"Nope. We had to make a food run or we couldn't go out, and you were taking too long. I told Dani I would hide her clothes so she couldn't go if she didn't eat something first. No repeats of last night on my watch."

Dani rolled her eyes. "I swear I'm going to start calling you 'Mommy' if you don't knock it off. And there is a 'Dearest' to follow that if you say one. more. word. I said I would eat. Your 'watch' is over."

Abi gave herself a swift mental kick at the revelation. She decided she really needed to get her act together. The downward spiral at jumping to the worst possible conclusion had her up to her eyeballs in the outhouse hole of her mind faster than she would have thought was possible.

They sat on the floor eating pizza and laughing. It was a light moment and Abi stuffed as much of it as she could grab down the throat of her inner demon. Even Dani was having a piece of pizza, though she had a sandwich with lettuce leaves instead of bread first. It was a compromise, but it was one that was going to actually get them out the door to the club.

The other three made their respective treks through the shower and not. The mirror got increasingly crowded as Abi finished her curls and the others began. Before she realized she was done, she was helping Margo get into a form fitting blouse of gold that set off her incredible curves. Norma Jean would have been jealous.

Dani had spent the majority of the time crimping waves into her hair in front of the dresser mirror. As Abi watched her, she decided that whatever Dani was wearing was evidently the accessory and the hair was the main feature. It was tedious to observe the extensive prep, she couldn't imagine the leaden arms she'd have to do her own hair, never mind Dani's much longer locks.

Meredith had emerged from the shower and was getting dressed as Abi helped Margo with a high, tight knot in her hair. With the deep tan, gold top and high hairstyle she looked all glamor. Abi was in awe.

"You my dear, are gorgeous!" Abi declared when the last hairpin was placed.

"Thanks. I…you know what? No, just thanks." Margo replied before she moved over to the bed to get her shoe situation on track. Abi noticed Margo had actually brought a pair of boots to wear. Not the new pair, and not as fancy as the new pair either, but a mid-calf, low wedge boot that was kind of dressy but might still give her support.

"You're not wearing the boot-boot tonight?" Abi asked from across the room.

Meredith and Dani turned to look at her as she responded. "I really don't want to. I probably should. I just want to look nice for the night instead of like the gimpy tag-along."

"Are you wearing pants or a skirt?" Meredith asked.

"I brought both. I want to wear the skirt which makes the boot-boot jump out."

"How tight can you make the dress boot for support?" Abi finally asked after the room was quiet for a solid minute as everyone tried to find the 'right' answer to the dilemma.

Margo shrugged. "I can put another sock under it and it's pretty tight."

"Hard call." Abi said.

Dani turned around with the ominous black orb of truth in her hand. "We can ask Magic 8."

"No. This one is all on me or not." Margo replied.

Meredith stepped in front of Abi who was watching Margo debate the boot versus boot-boot. "Can you help me with my hair too?"

"Of course." Abi replied and followed her to the mirror in the bathroom. She helped Meredith put her hair up in a French twist with a low front swoop. Meredith was in a vibrant red strapless dress with a little black bolero jacket and a set of huge white pearls.

"You know that dress would be a knock out without the jacket." Abi said offhandedly.

"Yes, it would, but…" Meredith flipped the lapel back revealing the white garments showing above the dress underneath.

"Oh." Abi replied. She wanted to be delicate but at the same time had to ask too. "Could you not wear the garments?" she asked softly.

Meredith heaved out a hard sigh. "I've been asking myself the same question for the last hour."

"And?"

"And I think the nerves of taking them off might melt me in a pool of perspiration." Meredith admitted.

"Then leave them on." Abi said flatly.

"But I want to take them off too." Meredith popped from side to side with indecision.

Abi held up a finger in the reflection to Meredith. "Dani…" she called out. "We need you and Magic 8."

Meredith's eyes flew wide. "No." she said on a whispered exhale.

"Hear the question first, you still have final say." Abi replied as Dani rounded the corner.

"What's up?" Dani asked.

"Shake please." Abi responded.

As Dani started shaking, Abi looked at Meredith and asked the question. "Will Meredith be compromised in any way if she takes off the garments for tonight?"

Dani flipped the 8-ball over. Meredith and Abi clunked heads as they tried to angle to see the response.

Very doubtful.

"Shake it again." Meredith said to Dani who flipped it back over and started shaking.

"Are you certain?"

Another flip, this time with no head collisions.

You may rely on it

"Thank you Dani." Meredith said.

After Dani went back to the other mirror to finish getting ready, Meredith looked at Abi over her shoulder in the mirror.

"This is crazy. Did I really just ask a Magic 8-ball for permission to take off my garments?"

Abi giggled softly nodding. "Yes you did."

"Do you think I dare?" her eyes were wide as she looked in the mirror at Abi.

"You're the only one who can answer that. It's your

revolution remember?" Abi replied quietly trying to let Meredith ease into the decision. "What you do or don't do when is up to you. I've got your back whatever the choice is."

Meredith looked herself up and down in the mirror several times. Abi didn't speak. Somewhere in this moment Meredith was taking a step or planning one and it was hers to make alone.

She watched silently as Meredith had the jacket on and took the jacket off. On, off. On, off…the debate was not hard to determine by what was going on.

When Meredith finally spoke, it was not an answer but a question. "Can you fix my hair again in a few minutes?"

"Yes, I can do that."

The next few minutes were the jacket on and off again with the hair up followed by on and off again with the hair down. Abi could no more tell what the verdict was from minute to minute as Meredith switched back and forth.

Meredith finally stopped, grinned wide and whispered. "Viva Zapata!" as she took the jacket off one last time.

Abi squeaked back, "Viva la Revolution."

Ask again later

Dani stuck her two middle fingers in the sides of her mouth and whistled for a cab. Margo had opted for the dress boot with an extra sock to keep it tight. She was parked against the building with instructions not to move until they got into a car. They were all going to be 'white on rice' over her for that ankle until they got back later tonight, and had each said as much.

Meredith was standing beside her, all rat pack glamour in a stunning red dress that she had covered up with a black trench coat at the last minute as they had left the room. No one had said a word about it, though it was really too warm for the coat, even for November. Abi was back and forth from the curb to the building in a silver tank blouse over black gauze, billowy pants and higher heels than Dani would have ever worn out on an uncarpeted surface. Her feet were going to hurt later, Dani was sure.

The driver whipped up like he was in a race to catch the fare though there were no other cabs in sight. The four of them piled in, giving Margo the front seat this time. Arriving at The Palms, they exited to a large early crowd. Meredith turned back to the driver before he pulled away.

"Do you have a card?"

"A what?"

"Can we call you when we're ready to go back? Do you have a card for that?" she asked the driver.

He fished a card out of the console. It wasn't his, but he scribbled his number on the back and handed it to her. "Call this number and I'll come get you. Give me a heads up and I'll even be waiting. I'm driving 'til four though, so after that you're in line with the rest of the crowd."

"Perfect. We'll call when we're ready." She replied with a smile.

"That was really smart." Abi said shoulder bumping her as they went in.

"Thanks. I can get it right on the first try sometimes too." Meredith ribbed.

"Pfft. Whatever."

The group stopped and took photographs under the neon bunny and 'Moon' signs that hung over the drive up to the club. There were several puddles along the walkway where the air conditioners were obviously running off and dripping down. They steered Margo around them as they made their way to the door.

Once inside, Dani made a beeline for the tattoo shop just off the casino floor. She walked in, made a large circle through the center looking into each of the stalls and was turning to head out when one of the artists stepped in front of her. They circled one another twice around.

"Looking to put some ink on that porcelain doll?" he started.

"Looking to add some ink to the porcelain. You any good?" she countered.

"I am. What are you looking for?"

"A Celtic knot with room for names later." She said.

"Hubby? Kids? How many letters are we talking about? That's tiny work." He scrutinized her request.

"Can you do it?" she asked flatly, not answering his question.

"I can do it."

"And I want a rose through the middle." She added.

"Black on black or color?"

"Greyscale except for the rose bloom." Dani countered commandingly.

"Yeah, I can do that."

"How much?"

"Six hundred."

"Six hundred?! Are you on crack?" she nearly jumped.

"This is Vegas, are you?"

Dani scoffed. "Not hardly. Six hundred is highway robbery for what I'm asking to have done. I wouldn't pay half that much."

"Then you realize you won't be getting it done here momma." He emphasized the two syllables of the last word.

Dani got up in his face. "If your price wasn't the deal burner, your attitude was. Good luck with that."

"This is Vegas baby, I'm in demand. Put up or walk away pretty girl."

"Walking here." Dani edged him out of her way and stepped out of the shop.

Abi was slack-jawed watching the exchange. "I didn't know you wanted to get a tattoo."

"I have a tattoo. I wanted to know what the going rate was for a piece I want to add. He's way off the mark price wise and his ego is a lot too big for my patience."

"So what's your tattoo?"

"It's a rainbow Playboy bunny." Dani laughed out loud. "How ironic huh?"

"Oh my gods, really? Let's see it then." Abi demanded tapping her foot, impatiently waiting.

"Yeah. I'll show you back at the hotel. I think, even though it's Vegas, they might kick us out if I dropped my pants in here." She snorted.

They sat at a long line of slot machines waiting for Raven and Vera to arrive. Margo was dropping coins and pulling the units arm from her perch on the stool with her leg tucked carefully between her and the machine. More than once she let out a rough curse and everyone looked to make sure it was that she'd not won or something, not that she'd hit the leg.

Several groups of young men passed and sized them up while they were waiting. Meredith pulled the tie on her trench coat tighter with each passing glance. Margo just ignored them.

Raven and Vera walked up a bit later. Abi's jaw dropped to see Raven in a black wrap dress with a deep V-neck front. Her silhouette was incredible, as was her cleavage. Several men followed them in. Dani laughed as one circled Raven and another walked up to Vera.

"Has anyone told you that you have eyes like Vivian Leigh?" he opened.

Vera snorted openly. "No. Does that line usually work for you? I doubt most of the girls in here know who Vivian Leigh is."

He held up a hand, "Guess you got her attitude too."

"Walk away little boy, you don't want to tangle with me." She retorted.

"Walking."

Dani turned just in time to see Raven pointing after the man walking away from Vera to one of his friends.

"What happened there?" Dani asked after he had moved off.

"The fingers between the hundred he was trying to slip into my dress almost got broken." Raven announced. "He said he thought the ring was just for show, his was. I told him where he could stick his ring and his hundred, and sent him to wingman his friend."

Abi clapped. "You go girl."

The next group of vultures lined up to pass. The leader kicked off. "Hello ladies. Any of you single looking for a good time?"

Meredith turned away. Margo, Raven, and Abi held up wedding ring clad left hands and Vera just shook her head no. Dani turned to tell them to push off but was whisked up in a twirl and dip move before she made it all the way around.

Her dance partner was shouting at her as he got a good

look. "You're Danica Marvel. Thank you Lord! Be still my heart. You know we could take some pictures that would really sell magazines."

Dani popped up and nearly head-butted the guy who let go of her quick. "Thanks, but no thanks."

"Your loss."

"Oh I very highly doubt it but you keep telling yourself that when you jack off to my picture later."

"I guess it's true. Just another pretty face. Now we know why you're single. Come on boys." He said to his entourage of wallflowers as they moved to leave.

Dani was seething. It took less than a second for her retort. Unfortunately, it was to their backs as they walked away. "Whatever lets you sleep at night jackass. Even on your best day you wouldn't have rated a drink."

She turned to the group. "Are we ready to go up? I don't think I can stomach any more of the bottom feeders down here."

As they walked, Vera commented to Abi. "You should have all kinds of material for your books after this."

A group of barely twenty-something girls were passing the

other way. One of the stepped in front of their group. "One of you is a writer? Which one? Do we know you? Can we be in your book?"

Abi rolled her eyes. "Obviously you don't know me if you don't know which one of us it is. No, you can't be in the book unless I need a character to kill off. We're on vacation, so no work talk. Thanks for stopping. Buh-bye."

Dani roared and gave her a hug from behind. "Thank you for that. I was beginning to feel like the only one doing the verbal Vegas bitch routine. I need a drink and you just earned one."

"Earned one?" Abi said canting her head to the side to look at Dani.

"Yeah. Earned one. That's the first time since we got here that the writer thing came up and you stepped up and said 'Yes I'm a writer.' like you meant it instead of choking or shying away from the question like you weren't sure. I'm proud of you."

The line was around the corner. It took them several minutes to figure out that they were in the line for Moon not for the Playboy Club. For a couple long moments Dani had panicked a little at how long it would take for them to get in, and if she would survive waiting in this crowd. She had finally gone to the head of the line to ask and was informed of the situation. Her relief was audible.

She went to get the rest of her group to change to the area for the club they had come for. As she walked back down the line she heard it all. The women commenting on if she was real or silicone, the men who wanted 'to get a piece of that', the ones that knew her and were jabbing friends to snap a picture quick, and the ones who had no idea and were telling companions what beautiful babies they would make with her later given half the chance if she weren't out of their league.

It was always the same thing, this was just a bigger cesspool of comments. Only the people were different, everything else stayed the same. Another stop light, different cars. New salt, old wounds.

She decided as she neared her group that people left their filters home when they came to Vegas. Nothing else explained the constant rude behavior. There was usually one in the crowd wherever she went. Here, there seemed to be a crowd of them with perhaps a lone exception that didn't speak their every thought out loud.

She was surprised to see Abi holding Meredith's trench coat when she reached them finally. She smiled openly as she caught sight of Meredith's nervous twitching. Crowd or no crowd, things were about to get interesting and she wouldn't miss it for the world.

As I see it, yes

They were waiting in the elevator bay lobby to go up. There wasn't a line, but the car was not fast to come. The shiny brass bunny to the right of the car designated which one they wanted. As they waited, Abi noticed Dani's profile mirrored in the brass, even in reflection she was stunning. It just wasn't fair somehow she mentally shouted, shaking her head as she lifted her camera to catch the image.

She listened politely to the conversation happening around her. The group was chatty about everything and nothing. Her inner voice was doing its best devil on her shoulder routine. She was buckling under as the car finally arrived and it was too late to do anything but get in with the group.

Ding

As the elevator chimed its arrival, Andrew Archer looked up. He always glanced up to see the new guests. It was a game he played with himself to see if he could guess the orders by the look of the patrons exiting the car. He was seldom wrong or off by much anymore, but the game had not lost its entertainment value. After years of serving drinks and observing, he found he was pretty good at reading people. It was also a great distraction to break up the landscape that came with being a bartender at a flesh club where there was usually a decent chance that a guest had on less than the wait staff, and they were basically in swimsuits with a tail.

He'd been tending the bar near the incoming elevator at the Playboy Club in Vegas for more than a year. Tips were good. Flesh was willing. He was happy.

He'd been plenty happy at his last gig, a relic down on Freemont Street whose glory days were more Rat Pack than now. This was the big time; bigger fish, bigger tips, bigger…everything. The bunny suits walking around weren't too shabby either.

His given name was Andrew, but anymore he answered to many others; hey you, buddy, bartender, double-A, Arch, Archer, Sir – though that one always cracked him up and made him look for his dad, and to his friends…Drew. Back in the day at the frat house, it had been Opie, but never

Andy. The Nevada sun had buried the freckles beneath a deep tan and age had taken the red deeper to an auburn that looked chestnut in the low light of the club back bar. Opie was officially dead.

As a student of humanity, he considered himself above average. He was definitely a hear learner, not the read and retain type, which made him perfect for this job. Standing behind the turrets of his bar, in his club, he was laird and master of twenty-three and one half feet of prime Las Vegas real estate, coveted landscape in the land of 'look at me'. He'd faced blue collars and celebrities across the mahogany and brass battlements. At the end of the night he was always the last man standing. Some nights he was even the one leaving with the 'hot chick'.

His inner monologue was cut short as it was time to do his thing. Amid the sparse car were a couple martinis, a house merlot and a surprise he seldom experienced. At the back of the car, talking animatedly as they moved to exit, was a sextet of women, obviously together, laughing their joy openly at arriving to his world for the night. It was only after their orders that he realized he would not soon forget these women, he got nearly every one of their drinks completely wrong.

He had been nearly certain that he was looking at a Malibu & pineapple, a cosmopolitan, a gin & tonic, a shaken margarita, a rum & coke, and that bringing up the rear was a rare sighting…a cognac. As he took their orders it became increasingly hard to keep his jaw from dropping open as his scorecard had him batting negative from beginning to end. It was a first. He had never struck out six in a row, or five because the jury would be out for a long time on gin & tonic who asked for his specialty, never actually revealing her beverage of choice. He might be right, but would not know.

Malibu & pineapple was actually a vodka cranberry, and the cosmopolitan became a brandy Manhattan next. The margarita was way off as she requested a white wine, and the rum & coke asked for a Long Island iced tea, which was at least in the neighborhood but still wrong. Cognac made the count 'O' for six as she asked for a top shelf, aged, single malt served neat. Going back to the beginning, being extremely flustered by the string of misses, he returned to the first order and asked her to repeat herself, just in case she wanted to tip her hand, actually hoping he'd gotten one. Bless her heart, she leaned closer over the bar and repeated herself, loudly.

"Your specialty please."

Well damn.

Drew dropped his head and began gathering glasses for the order. He couldn't help but snicker and had to bite the inside of his cheek so not to laugh out loud. Looking up he pasted a smirk on his face, the best he could manage, before announcing to the group.

"I'm going to need to see some ID ladies."

As they began to fish wallets out from points unknown, he worked steadily on the drinks. He'd card and serve them all together instead of one by one. It was only fair. He couldn't quite put his finger on where he'd messed up his signals. When you work with people and pay attention, you learn. He thought he was a consummate master. He decided as he prepped, that he had gotten cocky.

"All one check or separate tonight?" He muttered out as he finished making a cranberry apple-tini. It wasn't his specialty, but in his flummoxed, addled brain at six misses, it was what he'd come up with.

"I got this round." Single malt scotch chirped from the far end.

"Alrighty-then."

The disparities kept coming as he carded. Long Island ice tea was Vera Davenport from the northern part of California. If that wasn't irony, he didn't understand the definition. It was only further compounded as white wine flashed ID revealing her to be Raven Whitley from Boston. It was Saturday night in Vegas, anything was possible.

Vodka cranberry was Danica Marvel from California which finally clicked where he knew her from, she was on more than one magazine he'd seen in recent months. He had guessed umbrella drinks and sunshine when he'd seen her, he was right about the sunshine anyway. It was an easy error but still an error, though now also a small victory.

His cranberry apple-tini was Meredith Grace from upstate Utah. She was hiding her cards behind his 'specialty' drink. He wondered if it would stay that way or if she would tip her hand at the re-order. There was still time for him to get one right, the night was young.

Margo Upton was the brandy Manhattan and she definitely was. The balance between the sweet and the bitters just beneath the surface came out as drinks were served and the shifting around started. She was no-nonsense and not the cocktail glass flair Cosmo he'd misjudged her to be at arrival.

Knowing he'd struck out, he looked to single malt scotch at the end of the bar. Her ID said she was Abigail Stewart from Chicago. Her reserved demeanor said she was uptown, or life hardened. He would guess uptown. What cognac was to brandy, scotch was to whiskey, and aged single malt was royalty. She carried herself with a self-assuredness that resonated, but not the sometimes arrogance that he'd mistaken her for as cognac. There was something more too, but he'd have to wait for it. She was a cool customer.

He picked up his earlier train of thought as he served the last drink. He knew well how to learn people and he was feeling like he had a lot to learn from this group, all he had to do was listen. The world was his oyster with limitless possibilities if he paid attention. This was Vegas after all, what happened here as the saying goes...but sometimes what happens in Vegas can't stay. He ran single malt's card for the round, made the run of refills at the other end, and leaned back against the sink to be schooled.

Being surprised was a strange thing. Being able to read people and anticipate their wants had kept him in a higher rent district in a town where the room for a new slum lord could open up on a bad night. He'd gotten most everyone else right before this group, he simply had to know more about them. That, and he was always a sucker for a pretty face, here sat six.

As a bartender in Sin City, he'd heard everything. He'd been pretty sure he'd heard it all and then some too until cranberry apple-tini held up her drink to toast her friends.

"To the Zapatistas."

He damn near dropped the highball he'd just washed when he caught her words. He bobbled it again when the rousing 'Viva la Revolution" rang up from three of the others. James Bond couldn't have double-o'd his grey matter faster. *Revolution? Were they serious?* The group had clinked glasses giggling before getting up and ambling off into the club proper. As he watched, all but scotch took turns for a photo op with one of the fluffy tail clad waitresses before they got far.

Watching them was a study in stepping beyond boundaries. Each in their own way had moved beyond the person he had just seen at the bar. Vodka and apple-tini were pop-locking with a security guard behind the card tables without his knowledge. Drew could only think that was a good thing. He was friendly with all of the bouncers but that was one he didn't mess with ever. Brandy and scotch had taken up residence in the zebra thrones along the west wall until the floor manager came and booted them off.

Eventually the group found the stairs that led above to the open air bar and the dance club Moon. He lost track of them for quite a while then, but like all patrons who go up, they came down, resurfacing at the bar for refills. This time, he got it right and scored marks in the win column. So what if he struck out the first time up?

He tallied up a big tip and gleaming smiles when he lined up ice water next to their drinks. Being good at his job and maximizing his residuals may keep him in the lifestyle he wanted, but the smiles kept him in the frame of mind to appreciate it. The night was shaping up to be bonus territory all around.

It was a clear November night and he sure by the overflow crowd inside, that the dance floor above was packed. Lucky him. When the ladies finished gulping their waters and settled in to their drinks, he knew they were setting up shop for the night. Class was back in session.

Everyone was sticking to their original drinks, which was good for him. It was a great deal of work to remember orders in a changing crowd never mind when the orders changed for the same person. Their breathing had returned to normal and the silted silence ended as the wake of recovery ebbed. Not wanting to miss the opening volley, Drew jumped in first.

"So, Zapatistas eh?"

The fits of giggles and suppressed choking of a couple drinks stroked his soul. Scotch winked over the rim of her glass as the group raised them and responded to him, "Viva la Revolution!"

"Should I understand that?" he edged them to keep talking.

Apple-tini responded first. "Think of it as embracing our personal journeys."

"Y'all are from all over, where are we going?"

Scotch chimed in then. "Not where, to."

"There's a difference?"

She nodded back and him affirmatively. "There is."

"Ooooh, I love this song." Long Island interjected jumping up from her stool and heading off to dance followed by all but scotch who stayed put.

"Not your song?" he remarked offhand as they watched the group out on the floor.

"Not a dancer." She replied plainly. "Never really was my thing."

"What is?"

"Some days I'm not sure I know." She replied absently. He wasn't sure she meant to say that, or say it that way. She was lost in her own thoughts.

"Well that's cryptic. What's the journey to then?" he tried a different tack.

She shook her head coming back into the conversation before she began. "We each have something we're trying to do, or be, or become. That's the journey…to where we are that person." She cocked her head at the odd sounding sentence.

"And it's a revolution?" he prodded.

"It can be. Sometimes we have to remake ourselves to get to what it is that we are pursuing. That process is not necessarily easy, so ergo, a revolution." She summarized.

"That's pretty deep thought for Vegas. Most people come here to take their picture with the bunnies, but you didn't... Don't you want that souvenir?" As he got the question out he realized she was a student of humanity too. The why was eluding him, but she keenly watching everything happening around her, even as she spoke to him. He wondered if that was the look he wore as he watched and listened.

"No. Who I'm standing with in a picture is seldom of consequence. Mostly, they see them anyway, not me. I don't need the reminder."

"You know, sometimes it's not about who you're standing with, but who is standing with you." He tried to rally the conversation.

She sipped at her drink thoughtfully before responding. "Unfortunately, I find when I look it is more often than not that I am standing alone. The notion that I am standing with someone else, under the illusion that they in turn are standing with me, is not worth the lie."

He was stunned for a moment at the bluntness of her statement. It wasn't that it was cold, it was simply matter of fact. She harbored no disillusions that it was anything but what she saw as her reality.

"Have you stopped to look back?" he finally asked.

"Back? No. We don't gain ground backwards."

"You should. I don't know what your journey is about or where you are trying to be, but it seems to me that often when we stand on the precipice of something, especially when it is potentially something big, that it is not about who stands beside us, but who stands behind us.

The path forward is not always paved, or sometimes is only wide enough for one to walk. As the one taking the charge to go forward, or who is going 'to' as you say, there won't be anyone else in front of or beside us. They are there to make sure we don't fall. So, if we are to see them, we have to look back."

Her drink was half-way up when he finished. She set it down and stared at him long after the others returned to the bar for refills. He would love to know what she was thinking.

Refilling the other drinks up and down the bar, he didn't get the chance to ask before the group was up and gone. He hesitated a step at the vacant stools when he turned around. He wondered for a moment if he too should be on a journey of some kind. Perhaps another day he thought, discarding the idea before he realized that another day was already here. Sunday morning had arrived.

It is decidedly so

Meredith rode the high of the night out the main doors of The Palms and into the drive thru area. The neon lights glowed back at her from both ends of the arched canopy. It had been a great adventure.

Her joy was momentarily thwarted as she was nearly flattened by a group of, well groupies, trying to get to Dani. In the last moment as her own foot was being walked on, she shoved Margo behind her small frame to protect the less than protected ankle from being trampled. There wasn't so much as an 'excuse me.'

Looking down, she was more than a little heartbroken at the tread mark that crossed the toe of her red silk pump.

They hadn't been an expensive purchase, but an emotional one. In her mind the message was clear, no path is without its rocks, detours, or skid marks. At least this skid mark was not of her own making. She was pretty sure there were going to be more than a few of those along the way.

Dani held up a hand and uttered a single sentence. "Not tonight guys."

The group that had all but run to reach her sagged but not before someone had thrust a camera into Abi's hand with a "Take my picture" command. Abi calmly handed the camera back, but the sag in her shoulders matched those on many in the crowd grumbling away. Meredith watched Dani's face as she visibly hesitated giving in to the crowd before bucking up and sticking to the spot she stood. A heckler from the back got his jab in anyway.

"Come on Dani, you can do a few snaps. We know you're going home alone tonight, there's no man candy on that arm. Or, are these your girrrl-friends?" He drew out the innuendo he was making for the benefit of the audience around him who laughed.

Dani's jaw was ticking madly. She was obviously weighing very hard how to respond. Meredith wanted to interject but knew it wouldn't help, Dani had to face this one alone. Good, bad or otherwise, it was going to be a public moment, the price of being a public figure.

When Dani finally responded she did so in her most cool, calm, collected voice. It was the one that she reserved for interviews, the rude, and the uneducated. She spoke very slowly and used small words. Meredith had come to love this voice and tactic to make a point without making a scene ugly.

"Yes sir. These are my friends. They happen to be women, not girls, but potato-potato. Perhaps one day you too will have such amazing people to share your time with. I count myself very lucky. Thanks to the rest of you who understood that I was off the clock and enjoying a rare night away from the cameras. Be careful out there. Have fun. Good night." Her 'good night' had been commanding.

With her statement complete she turned away. Vera's family had just pulled up and she was leaving. They were dropping Raven off on the way, so Raven was departing too. They all traded hugs and waved goodbye just as their cabbie pulled into the drive.

The valet from the head of the line at the end of the drive whistled to the cab and called him over. The driver shook his head no and pointed to their group. Meredith had called as soon as they had exited the elevator so they would have time for goodbyes. The timing had actually been perfect.

The valet walked over to the cab and kept trying to motion him over to the line where other patrons were waiting for a ride. The driver vehemently shook his head no as the group of women moved toward the car. Meredith yanked her cell phone from her clutch and pulled up the calls screen before walking around to the driver's side of the car and showing the valet the image on screen.

"I called him. This is my cab. You may not have it. If the people in line did not have the forethought to call for a ride, let them wait in line for one to arrive. I am not giving up this ride because you say so. I am not waiting in line either. Now kindly stop harassing the ride I procured for my friends and me." She announced loudly enough that the crowd had stopped muttering and was watching what would happen next.

The valet was wide-eyed in disbelief. He waved the cab and Meredith off before returning to his post, flagging the next cab in to the head of the lineup. Meredith grinned over the top of the cab to her friends, "Let's go." From the crowd, some guy she couldn't see whistled and shouted to her. "Hey red dress…call me a cab and get me out of this line."

"Good luck with that buddy. Next time you'll know better." She shouted back feeling like she was powerful for the first time in a long time. His comment finally finished processing in her mind and she glanced down in shock to realize she was out in the open in her dress. She couldn't remember what she had done with her coat. She also realized that she hadn't missed it the last few hours since handing it off earlier in the evening.

She shot a dazzling smile to Abi on the far side of the cab. Magic 8 or no Magic 8, she had been out, without her garments, and in thinking it through, nothing had happened. She had not compromised herself, morally or physically. She'd had fun and, if she did think so herself, looked amazing while doing it.

Her face fell quickly as she watched Margo step off and slide through a puddle of standing water. The twist of the ankle, even with the tight boot for support was obvious from across the drive. She hadn't caught Margo's face as it happened, instead it had been a slow motion movie as she watched the step into the water, the slide, the twist, the bobble, and finally the hopping on the other foot with the damaged one up behind her crooked at the knee.

Meredith didn't swear, never really had, even as a rebellious teenager, if you counted makeup and broken curfews, she hadn't made that leap. She surprised herself to hear it come from her lips when the harsh "DAMN IT!" came out unbidden. Margo's foot had barely gotten off the ground before Abi and Dani were under her shoulders holding her up. Meredith was racing to reach the group.

"Please tell me it didn't crack or break." She launched as soon as she was within easy ear shot.

"I didn't hear anything, but I definitely rolled it." Margo

responded sounding like she was fighting tears.

"We got you. The cab is here. Into the back seat with you. You can put the foot up easier." Meredith was all orders and no argument.

She was not paying the least bit of attention to what else was happening around her as Abi and Dani helped Margo into the backseat and got in to support the ankle for the ride. Meredith didn't even notice as she climbed into the front seat that she had until she looked back to see Abi smiling at her. She didn't say it out loud, but mouthed her surprise to Abi instead. "I'm in the front."

Dani and Margo were talking trying to reposition her leg as Abi replied back, mouthing soundlessly. "I know. Twice in one day." She actually spoke then as she added, "Do you want your coat back now?"

Meredith thought for a second before answering. She stunned herself more than a little when the answer was "No. I'm good."

She turned back to face the front and clicked the seatbelt into place. It was not that the view was different so much as the symbolism of her moving up that made it the best ride of her life. She had felt like a second class, not quite good enough or arrived person for so long, she never expected anything more.

As she watched the sights go by she expanded her thoughts

to the dress and the evening. She was amazed to realize that as the night neared the end, she had no lingering guilt about not wearing the garments. Sure, she had been a little beyond her comfort zone, but she had also been within her own control, her own power, and acting guided by her own moral compass too. She was not behaving a certain way because she had on 'God's holy underwear' to remind her how to be. She knew how to be, and she had managed just fine.

She kicked her head back against the headrest and closed her eyes for a moment. One more piece was falling into place and she wanted to relish the moment. When they had all decided to meet in Vegas, she'd been more than a little hesitant. She heard the stories, or the lack of stories since what 'happened here, stayed here'. Never had she imagined that this trip would not only show her the path to achieving so much, but would also ground her to know that she could walk it.

There was a bit of euphoria at the idea of finally being free to be herself and not have to cling to something that was no longer serving her because it was the only way to be there for Jamie. How she was going to manage it, she really didn't know. What she did know was that however it worked, she could do it.

She was stronger than she had let herself be for so long. She knew that now. Screw the little black dresses and secret white garments, she should have put on a little red dress years ago.

Signs point to yes

Margo hopped down the hall toward their room between the supporting shoulders of Abi and Dani. Meredith was bouncing ahead of them with the key. Walking in, they deposited Margo on the bed nearest the door as Meredith ducked back out to the ice machine with a couple plastic bags from yesterday's shopping excursion.

It was late. Or, it was early depending on which day you were using for reference. Yesterday seemed like a distant memory. She had hoped yesterday. Yesterday she had determined that she could do things for herself for a change and it would all be okay somehow. How quickly the tide had turned. Today was a new reality.

She had decided less than twelve hours ago to wear a dress boot for herself and here she was with her foot up again, waiting for her friend to return with bags of ice. *Stupid, stupid, stupid.* The inner mantra echoed in her head. It was never going to end.

As she watched, her friends carefully unzipped and pealed the dress boot from her leg. The mottled yellow was still there. The swelling was already starting to creep up her leg. She couldn't hold the tears. Not because she was in pain, but because she felt like once again she had failed.

Dani sat down beside her and wiped her tears with a tissue from the night stand. "Is it hurting?" she asked softly.

"My pride. My ego. They hurt. The ankle does not compare to those." Margo replied with a hitched breath.

"Margo it could have been any of us." Dani consoled.

"Yeah, it could have been but it wasn't. It was me. Once again, it was me."

"This too shall pass and you know it. Let's get it iced down and then get the boot back on to stabilize it for the night. Come morning I'm sure it will just be memory." Dani remarked dotting the tissue at the tears that continued to sneak past before Margo could get her hand up to wipe them away.

"I'm just so angry." Margo confided. "I knew better, but I just pushed forward like I always do."

"Yeah, you're a bit of a stubborn cuss. It's really what's holding you back you know. You never let yourself be injured long enough to heal, so you never get out of the cycle." Dani remarked.

Meredith returned with the bags of ice. She took two towels from Abi and set them under the leg before putting the make shift ice packs on. They were sure to leak, and sleeping in a cold wet spot was not going to help. She walked off then and went to change out of her red dress.

Dani was changing too as Margo watched the trio move about as though nothing had happened. As though her ego had not suffered a major blow by a puddle of water, they were milling around the room. Abi cornered Dani.

"Let's see it."

"What?"

"The tattoo...hello, you're dropping trewes to change right? Let's see it." Abi commented smartly.

Margo laughed at Abi's demand and forgot the leg for a minute.

Dani turned around and eased the waistband of her lounge pants down. Sitting just below where the waistband of most pants would fall was a rainbow Playboy bunny with a bowtie, just like the club props from earlier in the night.

"Well I'll be." Abi laughed. "I thought you were yanking my chain. So whose names are going in the Celtic knot?"

Dani looked at her and sat on the edge of the bed. "It's just a dream of mine. I thought if I created the space for it, maybe I'd be motivated to take the step or somehow closer to having it."

"Having what?"

"A family."

Margo jumped into the conversation. "You have a family. You were born to one. And, we are your family too."

"It's not the same. The first is blood and that only goes so far when there's nothing beyond the DNA. The other is nice, but not what I want. I want more."

"I knew it! So go get it. Go do it. Family is a choice too…you say it like you can't have one." Margo was getting louder with each word. She had been very actively creating a family unit. She had known too well what it felt like not to have one, though she wasn't telling that little piece of the tale.

Meredith came around the corner from the bathroom. "What are you yelling about?"

"I'm not yelling."

"Yeah. You are. You don't have to f…" she paused stumbling for a word, "…freaking raise your voice to be heard." She quipped.

Margo dropped her volume. "Is this better? Can you hear me now? And, as long as we're talking about what we do and don't have to do, you know you're a big girl, you can use the

"F" word."

Meredith got red faced. "There is no need to cuss."

"You're leaving the church. You know it and I know it. There's nothing keeping you from an outburst every once in a while. You don't always have to be so in control and the goody-good."

"I never needed the church for that. I don't need the church to be a good person. And, I don't need to cuss just because I'm not planning to stay to the church routines."

"Well hallelujah you finally figured that out. I've been trying to tell you that for weeks." Margo retorted.

"It wasn't yours to teach." Meredith hissed. "And on that note, you need to learn when to step back too. You're all about 'not on my watch' and 'white on rice' if this or that. Maybe you need to realize that you have limitations. You are not wonder-freaking woman. You are not invincible. You can fall and the world doesn't come apart because of it."

Margo was stunned silent for a few moments at Meredith's outburst. Dani and Abi were actively not saying anything. They were watching the tennis match between her and Meredith.

When Margo finally spoke again it was quietly. She hesitated twice before she got out the hardest question she knew.

"Is that how I come off? Is that why I don't fit in?"

Meredith sagged and sat on the bed next to Abi. "Margo you do fit, you just don't seem to be able to step back and blend. Friendship is a china shop of delicate balances. You are a bull. You are always trying to be the one in charge and dictating. We allow it because we do like you and do want you with us. It doesn't mean we enjoy it. Maybe that's harsh, but you don't hear it otherwise."

Margo looked at Abi and Dani. "Is that what you guys think too?"

Abi heaved a hard breath before beginning. "I'm not the best person to answer that. I think we are at different places in our lives and if I were in your shoes I'm not sure that I would be any different. In some ways I wish I was more like you. I used to be. I used to be okay to stand alone and not feel like I was forgotten. I used to be independent, and in charge, and took no excuses. Life happens and it changes you.

Maybe that's why the first night the whole revolution thing resonated with me. I need to take back my spot because otherwise I feel like I'm just watching it slip away. That makes it about me, not you. I have no room to judge."

Dani picked up as Abi finished. "I can't answer that any better. I want what you have. I don't know how to get it. I ache for it. Every biting comment about being another pretty face cuts me to the quick. How can I want to be a mom and have a family when no one sees me as anything more than a face on a cover?"

Margo couldn't believe it. She had thought other than a few hurdles here and there that her friends all had exactly what they wanted. "I guess we all have things that we still don't know about each other. I mean, I knew about Meredith's decision struggle before we got here, but the rest? Meredith you're always put together. You never slip. You never stoop. You do get really angry, and have a wicked temper as I've now seen, but in my mind it was just a simple decision that would be made when you finally figured out that it was a simple decision. I guess to you it wasn't so simple.

"And Dani", she continued as she turned, "I don't know what to say to you either. I've spent years building my family and cementing us together. My mom was never around. I swore I would never be like that. It's damn near killed me a couple times. Ruptured spleen a couple years ago, blown up appendix, broken ankles, broken elbow, the list goes on.

Every time something happens I swear it's going to be the last. Then something else happens and I'm angry because I broke the promise I'd swore to myself. You want this? You can't possibly. You should want something better than this." Margo sobbed a little at the hard truth coming out.

She sagged and took a deep breath, turning again. "Abi, you have no idea who you are. Or, you don't see yourself very well. You may stand alone, but not because you are forgotten or taken for granted. I think you get to stand alone because, at least when I see you, you don't need anyone else standing there to be who you are.

You are an easy friend who just rides the waves as they come. I've watched you this weekend and you are the steady calm in everyone else's storm, in my storm anyway. You laugh and joke and somewhere in there, if you've been having moments, I had no clue because you were being there for everyone else as they needed you. Not once since arrival have I noticed you turn away from someone else. You are a damned, freaking rock. It's just everyone knows it but you."

Abi, Dani and Meredith were all staring at her when she finished. The room was eerily quiet. It was really uncomfortable too before long.

"What?" Margo snapped under the silent pressure.

Meredith composed herself first and replied. "I think that might be the most I've heard you say all weekend."

"Yeah well, short of the actual 'I'm sorry' it was long overdue. I think we all need to see ourselves through someone else's eyes. It seems to me like we're all seeing distorted pictures."

Abi hopped up and went to her briefcase. Margo hadn't been sure why she'd brought one since it was not a working weekend, but who knew, maybe it was a writer thing. When she came back she handed each of them a piece of paper and a pen. When she sat down with hers she started to explain.

"We said the other night that we were revolutionaries right?"

Margo squinted an eye. "Yeah, I think I missed that part."

"Oh come on. I explained it kind of good. We all have things that we want to change. We all have goals. We all have things we want to let go of too. So, here's the deal. And, we can agree to share or not…that's up to each of us, but I think we need to know the goal specifically before we start or it's really no different than wishing for something to be different."

"I don't follow" Dani interjected.

"I'm suggesting we take a couple and write down exactly what it is that we want. It has to be something we can actually do or work on. Then, and this is where it's up to you to share, we can share them and help each other, or we can lock it away somewhere and hold ourselves to it, but we make a promise to do it and not quit "

"And if you don't know how?" Dani asked.

"Give me an example." Abi replied.

"Say that there is something that you don't know how to overcome?"

Meredith piped up. "Abi can I change your thing a little, or add something that might help Dani here?"

"Sure."

Meredith beamed. "Okay, so we write down what it is, maybe why it's a thing, and why we don't think we can. I know for me it took someone else seeing the situation and asking questions for me to see how to do it." She looked at Abi as she spoke. "It changed everything." She turned then to Dani. "Does that help?"

Dani nodded.

"No judgements?" Margo asked.

"No judgements." Abi said sternly. "I think that's how we got to where we are to begin with. But, that also means you can't judge yourself unfairly either."

They were quiet for a long stretch as each scribbled on their pieces of paper. Margo looked up more than once hoping that hers was not going to sound trite to the others. It seemed like such a simple thing on the surface and yet she hadn't been able to manage it on her own.

When the pens finally stopped moving they all stared at one another. Margo wanted to speak up but couldn't. She knew she needed help and wanted help, but she was terrified to reveal that she was unable to help herself. She had been lashing out for so long, stepping back was hard.

Abi finally cleared her throat. "It was my idea. I'll start." She took a deep breath and looked at her paper before she set it down.

"I have said all along that I want to be a writer, and I do. It isn't that though. I wanted to be a writer because I thought it would help me get back to who I think I once was. I thought it would force me to reclaim my drive and to find a way to stand on my own. I'm tired of working for someone else and feeling like I'm never getting anywhere. Being a writer, it would be all me. But, it would also be all me. Thus, it's a double edged sword.

It's a nice thing to say but the truth is I've never thought I could because I feel like I'm always on the outside looking in." She turned to Margo. "You said I was a rock. I don't feel like a rock. I feel like I'm the bug under the rock that keeps being squished as people climb over to get to something else. I feel invisible. I don't feel like people ever see me. They expect me to be there, but then it doesn't make a difference if I am or I am not because that's where it ends. I'm alone in a crowd.

Then, there's the 'I want to be good enough' thing, but I want to be better than good enough and I want people to notice. This is a hard journey because my head tells me all the time just how 'not good enough' I am and I want to quit. If people know I'm a writer it's a different spotlight and I don't know how to stand in it. I feel my legs give out before I can actually even get up to the stage.

I need you guys to not let me quit. I need you guys to keep

me moving and not let me just say I'm doing it. I need someone to see me when I fail and not let that be my story."

Margo snorted. "You are such a writer. I felt every bit of that. If you need someone to kick your butt, I'm really good at that. I can help."

Dani and Meredith were nodding. Dani added to Margo's comments. "You're not invisible Abi. I didn't think you needed anybody. You seem so strong on the outside. I'd love to be one of the ones who gets to see you through the hard times. I never knew you had them. I was jealous because in my mind you had it all together."

Abi snorted this time. "So far from together. I'm the poster girl for fake it 'til you make it. I just keep missing the 'make it' part."

Meredith put her paper aside as she started to speak. "Abi you helped me more than you know already just yesterday. I do see you. Let me return the juju. We all know now that my journey is about the church and leaving the church, but like you being a writer, it's about more than that too.

I am trying to find my way. Jamie is trying to find her way too and it is a path I have traveled. I don't want to see her fall into the same empty patterns I did. I know now because of you guys that I can do this. I can be the example for her without the ceremonies of religion. I think it's going to be hard because I have never felt like I was seen as being worthy unless I was doing what the church had taught me to do or be, and that was a sham because it made me a sheep, nothing more. Even my marriage was about how the church taught us that marriage should be. I felt like a second class citizen in my home, like I was not supposed to be anything else.

I became the dutiful wife and kept my thoughts and feelings buried because it was what was expected. I have learned to be loyal and I expect it in return. What I realized, is that I have always mistaken the routine as being the return. It wasn't. It was never more than a rote response, and here I have wondered why it felt empty. It did, because it was.

I need to not settle. I need to not fall back into the habits and routines that have been drilled into me for so long. I need you guys to remind me to speak my mind and that my opinion is valuable. I need to feel like someone hears me. I need to be the example for Jamie of what it means to be both part of the church and true to herself. I haven't been for me, I don't know how to do it for her. I'm going to try, but I'm scared to fail."

"One step at a time Meredith. I think that is how you do it." Abi said. "I'll be here for you whenever you need me. It sounds like we have parallel roads to walk."

Dani chuckled. "Here I am trying not to be seen. I can surely help you do the opposite. The hearing part not so much, I feel like no one hears me, so I obviously don't have that one down yet. They see me and assume I have nothing more to offer. Maybe we can share that part."

Margo chimed in. "I guess I was hearing you and didn't stop to figure out how to get my message across to you in return. I know I'm a bit of a bull. I'm going to be working on it if you can stand to have me in your corner too."

"I can do that. I'll take all the help I can get." Meredith beamed back.

Dani jumped in before she lost her nerve. Several sore spots were about to be exposed. "Here goes nuthin." She said as she put her paper down. She stared at it as she spoke.

"I was raised in a boarding school. My mom thought they could do a better job and shipped me off. I didn't fit in. I was chubby and had crooked teeth. The girls made fun of me because I cried for my mom, but my mom never came. I changed myself to stop the laughter.

I want a family. Michael wants a family too. I just figured I would never have one. It would be professional suicide and it would mean throwing away everything I had fought to become to get pregnant. I'm thin, I'm considered beautiful. Everyone assumes I have it all. Glamour lifestyle, cute boy on my arm, toys, money…all the traps, but that's all they are, traps.

No one sees me as anything more, or as having anything to offer. It's like they see I'm pretty and blonde and therefore dumb. I have been different people online just so others would maybe think I was smart if they didn't know who I was behind the screen. I've made a great life living a lie.

I want to be seen, but not for what I look like. I want to have kids that need me. I want to be a mom and have someone's name to put in my tattoo. I don't know how."

"Dani you do know how. You just have to decide what you want more." Abi said quietly. "You have to choose and stick with the choice. It's not easy. I'd bet the pressure will be really horrible too. But, I have seen you when you dig your feet in and you are tenacious. That is how you do it. It seems to me you have three moms here who can help you with the rest."

Meredith grinned wide. "Given the history lesson the other night, there is no way anyone who knows you would think you are dumb. Good grief, we're all sitting here at what unbelievable hour of the day," she glanced at the clock, "talking about our personal revolutions because you translated history based on an analogy from an old movie. You'll never be a dumb blonde to me."

"So you'll still be my friend if I balloon up and become a carb loading history quoter instead?" Dani mocked.

"Puhleeeze." Margo said from the far side of the bed. "Got curves here. They aren't lethal." The room was a chorus of laughter. When it finally died, Margo continued.

"Which makes it my turn I guess." She began. "I didn't come up with anything as profound as you guys did. I just want to be and stay healthy. I want that for me and for my family. I tell myself I'm going to, and then I end up broken again. I need you guys to be on me to take care of me. You know I won't do it myself. Or, maybe I know I won't do it myself." She frowned at the revelation she had as she said it.

"I feel like the master puppeteer who cut his own strings and can't hold himself up. I run circles around everyone to keep them on track and never quite have my own life in order. It makes me sad, but it comes out as anger. I have always felt like I'm part of the crowd, but apart from everyone at the same time. I direct and dictate but, how did you say it? I don't blend, which makes it worse. I want to be part of the group and actually feel like I belong. I want to be part of the fun group too not just the ones in the room.

I guess I need you guys to be the reminders of when I'm out of control. I never see it until I'm broken again. I don't want to live this way anymore."

"So you're giving us permission to 'white on rice' you?" Meredith mocked grinning.

"Unless you know another way."

"I bet between us all we can find one." Dani added quickly.

"I know that's right." Abi nodded. "We can do it all. Maybe not all at once, but we can do it.

I need you guys, and I have huge hopes for each of you too. Margo, I think we can work out a check in of some kind to keep you on track. No crabbiness back though when we do. I also think we need to come up with a reward for when some of this happens. First off though, we need to get you well. Starting now." She said looking hard at Margo.

All three of them moved in then. They pulled the ice packs off and once she was dressed helped her get into the boot. Meredith switched to sleep with Abi since Margo was being given no choice but to sleep with the boot on for the night after her hydroplane through the puddle.

She was about to drift off but sat up abruptly. "Dani…give Magic 8 a shake would you?"

Dani sounded groggy as she muttered something. The sloshing and splashing sound cut through the quiet room as Margo asked her question.

"Magic 8, will this work?"

Dani sounded more awake as she hit the flashlight button on her phone and read the answer aloud.

Signs point to yes.

Margo repeated it to herself as she watched the pale pink dawn light slip under the window shade and drifted off. 'Signs point to yes.'

Most likely

Dani was hazy. The circle from the bottom of the Magic 8-ball was impressed firmly in her cheek as she woke. She remembered the conversations from before sleep. They had crossed into her dreams.

Somewhere in the night she had decided. The lingering goose bumps up her arm reinforced the emotional chills she had at the unencumbered visions. She was walking away from her career hand in hand with Michael and a toe-headed toddler. She could hardly wait to tell him.

The shower was running. She hoped absently she hadn't been talking in her sleep. Michael had laughed openly at her one morning for doing just that. She had apparently muttered an entire grocery list in her sleep from her dreams.

Abi stepped out wrapped in a towel. She smiled at her as she walked past. Meredith too was already up.

"What time is it?" Dani muttered.

"Almost noon sleepy head, we need to get moving." Meredith chirped.

"Ugh."

Margo walked in from the hallway just then hanging up her phone. Dani hadn't noticed that she hadn't been on it all of yesterday that she could recall until just now. Margo's boot was on over her capris. Everyone was up but Dani.

"How's the leg?" She asked as Margo sat down on the end of the far bed.

"Actually not too bad. A little tight, but the swelling seems to be down this morning. I can't thank you guys enough for playing nurse last night." She replied.

"Glad we got it in time." Dani moaned rolling over as her stomach gave a loud growl. "Ugh, I need food."

Margo gave a loud laugh "Well there's something I never thought I'd hear from your lips. I was just downstairs. The egg café is open until two, we can do brunch if you move your butt."

"Mmmm, brunch sounds good." Meredith added. "Get moving Dani."

They were studying the menus at a four-top in under

twenty minutes. Dani noticed that the group was quickly putting their menus down and she was still deciding. Thinking there was no time like the present, she closed her eyes and stabbed the menu with a blind finger. Opening her eyes back up, she found that she had landed on fried zucchini sticks. Seems she wasn't going so far off the deep end from the word go as she feared. They were a vegetable after all.

As they waitress took their orders, she noticed from her peripheral vision the shocked looks that were buried quickly as she ordered.

"Did my ears deceive me or did you just order a flatbread and fried zucchini?" Margo asked.

"Gotta start somewhere I guess." Dani mocked. "I can't be the mom who does the health food all the time, my kids will hate me."

"You're a mom?" came a tiny voice from across the aisle. The little girl couldn't have been more than five. She was a Precious Moments look alike with fine little blonde pig-tails in her hair.

Dani grinned wide at her. "No sweetie. Not yet, but I'm going to be."

"My mom doesn't look like you." The little girl continued after her mom had shushed her. Mom was obviously doing her best to be invisible as she fed a smaller child in her lap and tried to hide the spill on her blouse.

"You're right. Your mom is doing much more than I am. I hope I look like her someday."

"You do?" the girl's eyes were wide.

"I do. Look how much she loves you. I can see it. Can you?" Dani asked.

The little girl looked at her mom and back at Dani.

"You know I really can."

"You're a very lucky girl."

"I know." The girl said sounding amazed.

"Better eat up or your brother is going to be done first." Dani said and turned back to see three stunned, smiling faces staring at her.

Margo leaned over to whisper to her, "Don't let our lack of good role models growing up deter you. If you have any doubts about if you're going to do it right, let me tell you, you are absolutely wrong. You're going to be great."

"Yeah? Well reinforcements won't hurt. I'm still holding you guys to having my back."

"You don't need to worry. We'll be there." Abi said.

"I was thinking, I heard this thing about if you write down your wishes and then burn them, it's kind of like sending them out into the universe to help you meet them. Do you think we should burn our revolutions?" Dani asked between bites after their food had arrived.

"I don't suppose it would hurt. I'm not sure how I'd

explain that to my family though." Margo said.

"We have a burn ban, but I don't see that it would hurt either." Meredith added.

"I think it's a great idea." Abi exclaimed. "I burn all the time back home. Another piece of paper isn't probably going to be noticed. I'll do it."

"Would you burn mine?" Dani asked.

"Sure."

Meredith and Margo chimed in together, "Mine too? Jinx."

"Gladly."

"Deal." Dani closed the subject.

Back in the room the packing was happening. Abi's flight was not until early the next day so she was staying behind. Dani was dropping the other two off on her way to head home.

Her air mattress did not want to compress down. By the end, all four of them were lying on it and rolling to get the last of the air out so it could be packed. They were all having attacks of giggles as they crammed and pushed to get it into the bag. "You know Dani you really could have just slept with one of us." Meredith finally said. "It would have been fine."

"And miss all this fun? No way." Dani mocked back.

As the bags stacked up Dani couldn't remember them hauling in so many and couldn't figure out where the extras had come from. Abi's were not even in the pile.

"I think that's everything." She announced.

"Hold up." Abi said.

The three turned as she stood staring at them holding a folder she'd pulled from her briefcase. She wore an odd expression for a long moment before she continued. "I need you to read this. Not now, but soonish. Don't tell me if it's terrible. I meant it when I said LIE." She swallowed hard. "You'll have to share it with these guys when you're done cuz I only have one copy. If I'm going to do this thing, I need to start walking the walk. It's only a hobby if I don't let anyone else see it right?"

"Is this a book?" Dani asked as the folder settled into her hands.

"It's the start of something I've been working on. I don't know what it is yet. A bunch of words, some rambling pages, or something more…I'm not sure. Just don't crucify me okay?"

Dani noticed that Abi had crossed her arms when the shake in her hands had become visible. Her fried zucchini seemed like such a tiny step in comparison. It wasn't, but she wasn't shaking like a leaf to have eaten. Abi was going to rattle apart standing in front of her.

"You sure you want me to read it first?" Dani asked.

Abi sat down on the edge of the bed before she answered.

Dani noticed she sat on her hands as she did so. It was a fairly smooth move, but since she'd seen the shaking she noticed it.

"I'm not sure I want anyone to read it. I almost didn't bring it at all." She shrugged. "I know if I don't now though, I never will. You guys said you have my back. It's time to trust fall and let you."

"I get that." Dani replied. "I really do." She looked at the others. "We all do." Meredith and Margo were nodding behind her.

Abi didn't say anything more but Dani watched her get herself under control before she stood back up. When she was fully up and settled she finally returned to herself.

"Since some of you, ahem…" she side glanced to Dani "over packed…would you guys like help getting all of this to the car?"

Dani plastered her best innocent face on. "Gosh, I thought you'd never ask. Of course we'd like help getting all this to the car. Margo can carry Magic 8 but the rest would be great to have help with."

"I get to carry Magic 8? Wow, are you sure that's okay for the juju?" Margo laughed.

"Oh, did I say Magic 8, I meant Magic 8's." Dani snorted out. "I got one for each of you to remember me." She added grinning madly.

"You're unreal. Do you know that?" Margo added reaching out for hers as she mocked. "Where's mine? I got a few questions I'd like to ask without you snooping my answers."

Dani handed her the bag after taking one out and handing it to Abi. "Ask your questions later, we need to get moving or we're going to miss departures and none of the revolutions are going to happen if we're stuck in Vegas. I don't need Magic 8 to tell me that."

Without a doubt

They dropped Abi off at the front drive of the hotel. Meredith didn't even care that she was once again in the backseat. Once Abi got out, she kicked her feet up across the expanse and stretched.

"I think you're right Abi, I could get used to be chauffeured around." She said with a wry grin out the window.

"I told you so. But first, you need to get your skinny ass up and give me a proper hug good bye."

Dani had thrown the car in park and climbed out. Her straw hat was bouncing up and down as her signature 'Nnn-cha' made it around the car ahead of her before she reached the curb side. Meredith jumped out and launched into Abi before Dani could reach her, spinning so her back was to Dani. "Nope. You got to wait your turn."

When she finally released Abi, Margo was standing in line for a turn waiting too. So much had happened in such a short window of time. None of them would ever be the same.

Meredith hopped back into the car and waited for Margo and Dani to have turns. It was going to be hard to say goodbye to the last of them. Even knowing they'd be back online chatting before they had time to miss each other, it wasn't going to be what this weekend had become. They were each leaving Las Vegas far different than how they had arrived.

She was actively not listening to the goodbyes, her eyes were watery already. She caught Dani's 'next time no air mattress' comment, and Abi telling Margo they would all be checking on her. They really were going to do this. It seemed surreal.

Dani and Margo each handed pieces of paper to Abi before they moved to get back into the car. Meredith sat up, leaned over the back seat and shuffled through the bags to grab hers. She'd nearly forgotten. Maybe it would be better if they each burned their own, but this was going to be close enough. The symbolism of it was the same. There would be no turning back.

Meredith stared down into her bag as she grabbed the

paper. Could she really do it? Her palms were sweating as she grabbed the other piece. Dani and Margo had both gotten back in and Dani had fired the engine back up.

"We ready to go?" she asked over her shoulder.

"Wait!" Meredith cried. "I've got to give Abi my paper."

"Hurry it up Meredith. The sun isn't going up anymore." Margo called back as Meredith hopped out again.

Abi was looking at her holding the papers in her hand. She had folded them together. In many ways it was as it should be that all their journeys go up together. They would never be embarking on them except for the events of the last three days and each other.

Meredith handed her paper to Abi and watched her fold it in with the other two. She hesitated the next move. She knew it was not a step she could ever take back if she made it.

As if Abi knew her, and she probably did now, she waited calmly for Meredith to take the next step, backward or forward, she wasn't pushing. Meredith looked back over her shoulder into the car. Dani and Margo were talking between them. This moment really was all about her.

She took a deep breath and let it out. With the second deep breath she brought her hand up and gave the white bundle to Abi. "Burn these for me too."

"Are you sure?" Abi asked softly.

"No."

Abi nodded. "Then you let me know. I've got you covered, whatever you decide."

Meredith mashed her lips tight and let the pent breath out through her nose.

"I'm scared." She admitted on a whisper.

"I know. Me too."

"Promise you'll be there?"

Abi smiled softly, "As long as I breathe."

Her eyes were starting to water. She had to get out of there or they were both going to be blubbering puddles on the sidewalk. Abi wore a face that she was sure mirrored her own.

She took a deep breath in through her nose, pulling back the tears that were trying to sneak out that way when her eyes refused to blink them free. Once she felt like she could talk without wobbling, she nodded and locked a hard stare on Abi.

"Then I don't need them anymore. Let them burn."

It is certain

Abi watched the SUV pull away into traffic. The early Monday morning flight had been cheaper than the Sunday night red eye. She would have twelve hours until her shuttle picked her up in the morning.

She had meant to go wander down Freemont Street when the girls dropped her off, instead she found herself rooted to the sidewalk holding three pieces of paper and Meredith's garments. It was not lost on her that in this moment she stood alone. It occurred to her as the thought crossed her mind, that from this moment on, she was never alone now. Not really. Her inner voice of venom was notoriously quiet for the first time she could recall.

Several loud horn blasts drew her attention. As she looked up she was overcome to see three fists out the windows of the disappearing vehicle just as "Viva Zapata" echoed back to her on the breeze. She threw both fists into the air, still clutching their plans and the underwear, shouting as loudly as she could in reply. "Viva la Revolution!" The tears she'd held for Meredith made a fast break at the opening and rolled down her cheeks.

More than one pedestrian's eyes went wide as heads turned. She was overcome by fits of giggles as she turned to go back into the hotel. What a sight she must be.

She carefully packed away the papers to burn and folded the odd garments before putting them in her luggage. Her shuttle was paid for, but would not wait if she was not on the curb at the designated hour. She was leaving nothing behind and made a double and triple check of the drawers, hangers, and bathroom before she set out again.

Down on Freemont Street she wandered through the pop up stands and shops. A different showgirl was out taking pictures. She hesitated. Remembering the bartender's words from the previous night about people you stand with, those who stand with you and those who support you from behind, she didn't need a picture.

She re-visited the gift shop from Friday night and picked up a few of the 'that mom' novelties to give her family. It didn't seem right to stick to the practical things anymore. It was time to do everything differently.

She got a sandwich from a street vendor and sat to watch the crowd. There was oblivious joy in many. In others she saw herself as she must have looked when she had arrived. They were the ones who were watching, waiting for something to happen. They were missing everything around them, worried about what might never be.

As she sat she realized that she was noticing things she had missed the other night. The smell of the open grill that reminded her of home. The sound of the Elvis impersonator wafting out from one of the casino stages that said she wasn't. And, the anthem of 'I'm proud to be an American' that was still blaring loudly, took on a more profound meaning than just background noise as she looked up and actually stopped to read the names of the men that had given everything for those they would never know.

It was a moment of perfect clarity at all the things she had missed, and not just here. She had surrendered so much along the way with 'what ifs' that she had stalled and never recognized that the fire had died. It was as though she woke up and everything was new.

She had, they all had, come to Vegas for an escape, a girl's weekend to get away from everything that they were facing every day. She never expected that she would get away to realize everything that was there in front of her face that she'd been missing because she hadn't been looking. She watched an artist making landscapes in paint from cardboard box sides and thought about the possibilities.

Her dad had always said the grass was always greener where they spread the manure. She decided he was wrong. Sometimes, the grass was simply greener because you stopped to actually see it. She amended her revolution to remembering to stop and see the world, not just live in it and hope she was seen in return.

She slept with her clothes on. Traveling had always been a confusion for her. When she was able to relax and take a lazy pace she was up with the sun. When she needed to be up, she invariably slept through the alarm. She set the clock on the night table, scheduled a wakeup call, set the alarm on her phone and tipped the shuttle desk to call her room at three-thirty to make sure she was up in time to be curbside at four for her ride back to McCarran. She had done some growing up here, but she was not staying.

She saw every hour as she tried to sleep and not oversleep at the same time. When the phone rang at three-thirty, as predicted she had missed both alarms. When it rang again at three-thirty-five, she jumped up, brushed her teeth, shoved the toothbrush in her briefcase, ran a washcloth over her face, grabbed her bags from next to the door, and was curbside at three-forty-five.

The coffee shop was not open. She could have used a jolt. As she looked around, Vegas was quiet.

Hours earlier, Freemont Street had been a bustle of activity with tourists. The casinos were still open, but there was little movement she could see. Not even the street had traffic. She was truly as alone as she had ever been. Somehow this time it wasn't paralyzing.

Reaching into her briefcase, she extracted the Magic 8-ball that was now all her own. She gave it a hard shake and watched the inner piece twirl and settle. She chuckled out loud when *Concentrate and ask again* came up.

As though it too saw the humor, her laughter echoed back from the empty street.

"Okay Magic 8." She began shaking it again before she continued. "I can do this, right?"

It is certain.

She stared at the answer and knew it was true. She nearly dropped the ball when her phone chimed a text. It was Meredith.

'Curb, shuttle or airport?'

Curb. Why are you up?

'Because you are. You ready to do this?'

Ready as I'm gonna be.

'You know you got this right?'

I'm nervous.

'I know. Me too. Remember you are never alone.'

Promise?

'As long as I breathe.'

Meredith returning her response from near this same spot on the curb twelve hours earlier restarted the tears. As if she needed to speak to type her reply, her breath hitched. Her eyes were too wobbly with tears to see the keys for a moment. She dashed them away before responding.

Then I got this.

'Viva la Revolution Abi!'

Her shuttle pulled up then. The next step was hers. She took one last look down Freemont and made a promise to herself, to never forget what she'd learned here. She reached down and grabbed her bag before stepping off the curb to whatever came next.

"One to the airport?" the driver asked as the door opened.

"Today the airport, tomorrow the world." She replied feeling light as she said it.

"Then climb in quick little lady, the world waits for no one."

Abi grinned at him as she took the first step up into the shuttle. He'd called her 'little'. She missed the middle of his comments but caught the end.

"It sounds like you've got a long road to travel before

you're done."

Abi winked as she handed him her ticket. "More than you know. Lucky for me I've already started. The beginning has been spectacular. I expect the rest to be even better."

She didn't say 'Viva la Revolution' as she moved to take a seat. She didn't need to. It was there, deep down inside, shouting all on its own when she realized, she'd meant every word. The journey really had begun. Her new future was here and she couldn't wait to keep going.

SAVANNAH VERTE

Upcoming titles from Savannah Verte

Bet the House

Red Bowerman knew where all the bodies were buried. This really wasn't saying much as a piece of his soul laid with each of them in their shallow graves a few feet under the Nevada sands. Regret would get him nothing now as the developers were moving in and soon all his ill-buried secrets would be revealed.

He has one chance to protect the past, but it could cost more than he is ready, or able, to pay. A single game in the casino would save it all, or could cost his home, his future, his heart, and perhaps his life. How much is it worth to keep a secret?

Book of Change

The history of the world, past, present, and future, resides in the pages of a single book. It is handed to the next Keeper each generation when the child of light appears. The book only remains constant for the chosen. For anyone else, something changes.

A seemingly random act leaves the book unguarded and it is taken. Can the book be recovered before it changes? Or, will the book fall into the hands of those who wish to use it to change the world forever? Only the book knows for sure.

SAVANNAH VERTE

ABOUT THE AUTHOR

A lifelong lover of words and reading, Savanah Verte hasn't quite figured out what she wants to write when she grows up, she hasn't found a story yet that she wouldn't tackle. For so many reasons thus, Savannah considers herself a 'Contemporary Vagabond' when it comes to writing and hopes that others find her diverse offerings as enjoyable to read as they are to write.

As one of the primary owners of Eclectic Bard Books she considers herself immensely fortunate to see writing from varied perspectives. Working with other authors, Savannah gets to expand her horizons every day as someone brings a new idea to the table and the brainstorming begins. There is something addictive about the creative process for her and helping other authors embrace their dreams make hers a reality daily.

www.ingramcontent.com/pod-product-compliance
Lightning Source LLC
Chambersburg PA
CBHW070836120626
46556CB00002B/776